"How do I stop them from finding Noah?" Marin asked.

"I won't let anything happen to Noah, understand?"

She shook her head. "I can't lose him."

"I know." And because he truly understood her concern and fear, Lucky reached out and slid his arm around her.

Marin stiffened, but she didn't push him away. Then she looked up at him, and he felt the hard punch of attraction. A punch he'd been trying to ward off since the first time he'd watched Marin and considered her simply part of his case. But she was more than that now.

Lucky couldn't lose focus. A knock at the door interrupted anything stupid he was about to say. Or do. Like kiss her blind just to prove the attraction that was way too obvious.

DELORES FOSSEN

SECURITY BLANKET

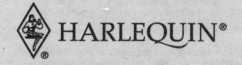

HARLEQUIN®

TORONTO • NEW YORK • LONDON
AMSTERDAM • PARIS • SYDNEY • HAMBURG
STOCKHOLM • ATHENS • TOKYO • MILAN • MADRID
PRAGUE • WARSAW • BUDAPEST • AUCKLAND

To the Magnolia State Romance Writers.
Thanks for everything.

ISBN-13: 978-0-373-69358-0
ISBN-10:   0-373-69358-3

SECURITY BLANKET

ABOUT THE AUTHOR

Imagine a family tree that includes Texas cowboys, Choctaw and Cherokee Indians, a Louisiana pirate and a Scottish rebel who battled side-by-side with William Wallace. With ancestors like that, it's easy to understand why Texas author and former Air Force captain Delores Fossen feels as if she was genetically predisposed to writing romances. Along the way to fulfilling her DNA destiny, Delores married an Air Force Top Gun who just happens to be of Viking descent. With all those romantic bases covered, she doesn't have to look too far for inspiration.

Books by Delores Fossen

*Five-Alarm Babies
**Texas Paternity

CAST OF CHARACTERS

Quinn "Lucky" Bacelli—The Texas P.I. who follows businesswoman Marin Sheppard onto a Dallas train in the hopes that she'll lead him to her fugitive brother.

Marin Sheppard—A trip home becomes a nightmare for Marin when a killer comes after her and her infant son. She has no choice but to trust Lucky, the bad boy P.I. who dropped into her life, even though Lucky might be the very reason she's in danger in the first place.

Noah—Marin's eight-month-old son.

Dexter Sheppard—Marin's brother has been missing for a year. His shady business ties are now haunting his entire family.

Lois Sheppard—Marin's overly protective mother who, along with her husband, is challenging Marin for custody of Noah.

Howard Sheppard—Marin's father. He would seemingly do anything to make sure his son, Dexter, never goes to jail for his criminal activity.

Brenna Martel—Dexter's lab assistant and former lover. She's missing and presumed dead, but did she fake her own death to escape justice?

Kinley Ford—Lucky's sister. She went missing during an explosion at Dexter's research facility.

Grady Duran—Dexter's former business partner. He's not afraid to use strong-arm tactics to find Dexter…and that includes threatening Marin and Lucky.

Chapter One

The man was watching her.

Marin Sheppard was sure of it.

He wasn't staring, exactly. In fact, he hadn't even looked at her, though he'd been seated directly across from her in the lounge car of the train for the past fifteen minutes. He seemed to focus his attention on the wintry Texas landscape that zipped past the window. But several times Marin had met his gaze in the reflection of the glass.

Yes, he was watching her.

That kicked up her heart rate a couple of notches. A too-familiar nauseating tightness started to knot Marin's stomach.

Was it starting all over again?

Was he watching her, hoping that she'd lead him to her brother, Dexter? Or was this yet another attempt by her parents to insinuate themselves into her life?

It'd been over eight months since the last time this happened. A former "business associate" of her brother who was riled that he'd paid for a "product" that Dexter hadn't delivered. The man had followed her around Fort Worth for days. He hadn't been subtle about it, either, and that had made him seem all the more menacing. And she hadn't given birth to Noah yet then.

The stakes were so much higher now.

Marin hugged her sleeping son closer to her chest. He smelled like baby shampoo and the rice cereal he'd had for lunch. She brushed a kiss on his forehead and rocked gently. Not so much for him—Noah was sound asleep and might stay that way for the remaining hour of the trip to San Antonio. No, the rocking, the kiss and the snug embrace were more for her benefit, to help steady her nerves.

And it worked.

"Cute kid," she heard someone say. The man across from her. Who else? There were no other travelers in this particular section of the lounge car.

Marin lifted her gaze. Met his again. But this time it wasn't through the buffer of the glass, and she clearly saw his eyes, a blend of silver and smoke, framed with indecently long, dark eyelashes.

She studied him a moment, trying to decide if she knew him. He was on the lanky side. Midnight-colored hair. High cheekbones. A classically chiseled male jaw.

The only thing that saved him from being a total pretty boy was the one-inch scar angled across his right eyebrow, thin but noticeable. Not a precise surgeon's cut, a jagged, angry mark left from an old injury. It conjured images of barroom brawls, tattooed bikers and bashed beer bottles. Not that Marin had firsthand knowledge of such things.

But she would bet that he did.

He wore jeans that fit as if they'd been tailor-made for him, a dark blue pullover shirt that hugged his chest and a black leather bomber jacket. And snakeskin boots—specifically diamondback rattlesnake. Pricey and conspicuous footwear.

No, she didn't know him. Marin was certain she would have remembered him—a realization that bothered her because he was hot, and she was sorry she'd noticed.

He tipped his head toward Noah. "I meant your baby," he clarified. "Cute kid."

"Thank you." She looked away from the man, hoping it was the end of their brief conversation.

It wasn't.

"He's what…seven, eight months old?"

"Eight," she provided.

"He reminds me a little of my nephew," the man continued. "It must be hard, traveling alone with a baby."

That brought Marin's attention racing across the car. What had provoked that remark? She searched his face and his eyes almost frantically, trying to figure out if it was some sort of veiled threat.

He held up his hands, and a nervous laugh sounded from deep within his chest. "Sorry. Didn't mean to alarm you. It's just I noticed you're wearing a medical alert bracelet."

Marin glanced down at her left wrist. The almond-shaped metal disc was peeking out from the cuff of her sleeve. With its classic caduceus symbol engraved in crimson, it was like his boots—impossible to miss.

"I'm epileptic," she said.

"Oh." Concern dripped from the word.

"Don't worry," she countered. "I keep my seizures under control with meds. I haven't had one in over five years."

She immediately wondered why in the name of heaven she'd volunteered that personal information. Her medical history wasn't any of his business; it was a sore spot she didn't want to discuss.

"Is your epilepsy the reason you took the train?" he asked. "I mean, instead of driving?"

Marin frowned at him. "I thought the train would make the trip easier for my son."

He nodded, apparently satisfied with her answer to his intrusive question. When his attention strayed back in the general direction of her bracelet, Marin followed his gaze. Down to her hand. All the way to her bare ring finger.

Even though her former fiancé, Randall Davidson, had asked her to marry him, he'd never given her an engagement ring. It'd been an empty, bare gesture. A thought that riled her even now. Randall's betrayal had cut her to the bone.

Shifting Noah into the crook of her arm, she reached down to collect her diaper bag. "I think I'll go for a little walk and stretch my legs."

And change seats, she silently added.

Judging from the passengers she'd seen get on and off, the train wasn't crowded, so moving into coach seating shouldn't be a problem. In fact, she should have done it sooner.

"I'm sorry," he said. "I made you uncomfortable with my questions."

His words stopped her because they were sincere. Or at least he sounded that way. Of course, she'd been wrong before. It would take another lifetime or two for her to trust her instincts.

And that was the reason she reached for the bag again.

"Stay, *please*," he insisted. "It'll be easier for me to move." He got up, headed for the exit and then stopped, turning back around to face her. "I was hitting on you."

Marin blinked. "You…what?"

"Hitting on you," he clarified.

Oh.

That took her a few moments to process.

"Really?" Marin asked, sounding far more surprised than she wanted.

He chuckled, something low, husky and male. Something that trickled through her like expensive warm whiskey. "Really." But then, the lightheartedness faded from his eyes, and his jaw muscles started to stir. "I shouldn't have done it. Sorry."

Again, he seemed sincere. So maybe he wasn't watching her after all. Well, not for surveillance any way. Maybe he was watching her because she was a woman. Odd, that she'd forgotten all about basic human attraction and lust.

"You don't have to leave," Marin let him know. Because she suddenly didn't know what to do with her fidgety hands, she ran her fingers through Noah's dark blond curls. "Besides, it won't be long before we're in San Antonio."

He nodded, and it had an air of thankfulness to it. "I'm Quinn Bacelli. Most people though just call me Lucky."

She almost gave him a fake name. Old habits. But it was the truth that came out of her mouth. "Marin Sheppard."

He smiled. It was no doubt a lethal weapon in his arsenal of ways to get women to fall at his feet. Or into his bed. It bothered Marin to realize that she wasn't immune to it.

Good grief. Hadn't her time with Randall taught her anything?

"Well, Marin Sheppard," he said, taking his seat again. "No more hitting on you. Promise."

Good. She mentally repeated that several times, and then wondered why she felt mildly disappointed.

Noah stirred, sucked at a nonexistent bottle and then gave a pouty whimper when he realized it wasn't there. His eyelids fluttered open, and he blinked, focused and looked up at Marin with accusing blue-green eyes that were identical to her own. He made another whimper, probably to let her know that he wasn't pleased about having his nap interrupted.

Her son shifted and wriggled until he was in a sitting position in her lap, and the new surroundings immediately caught his attention. What was left of his whimpering expression evaporated. He examined his puppy socks, the window, the floor, the ceiling and the ruby-red exit sign. Even her garnet heart necklace. Then, his attention landed on the man seated across from him.

Noah grinned at him.

The man grinned back. "Did you have a good nap, buddy?"

Noah babbled a cordial response, something the two males must have understood, because they shared another smile.

Marin looked at Quinn "Lucky" Bacelli. Then, at her son. Their smiles seemed to freeze in place.

There was no warning.

A deafening blast ripped through the car.

One moment Marin was sitting on the seat with her son cradled in her arms, and the next she was flying across the narrow space right at Lucky.

Everything moved fast. So fast. And yet it happened in slow motion, too. It seemed part of some nightmarish dream where everything was tearing apart at the seams.

Debris spewed through the air. The diaper bag, the magazine she'd been reading, the very walls themselves. All of it, along with Noah and her.

Something slammed into her back and the left side of her head. It knocked the breath from her. The pain was instant—searing—and it sliced right through her, blurring her vision.

She and Noah landed in Lucky's arms, propelled against him. But he softened the fall. He turned, immediately, pushing them down against the seat and crawling over them so he could shelter them with his body. Still, the debris pelted her legs and her head. She felt the sting of the cuts on her skin and reached out for something, anything, to use as protection. Her fingers found the diaper bag, and she used it to block the shards so they wouldn't hit Noah.

The train's brakes screamed. Metal scraped against metal. The crackle and scorched smell of sparks flying, shouts of terror, smoke and dust filled the air.

Amid all the chaos, she heard her baby cry.

Noah was terrified, and his shrill piercing wail was a plea for help.

Marin tried to move him so she could see his face, so she could make sure he was all right, but her peripheral vision blurred. It closed in, like thick fog, nearly blinding her.

"Help my son," she begged. She couldn't bear his cries. They echoed in her head. Like razor-sharp daggers. Cutting right through her.

Sweet heaven, was he hurt?

There was some movement, and she felt Lucky maneuver his hand between them. "He's okay, I think."

His qualifier nearly caused Marin to scream right along with her son. "Please, help him."

Because she had no choice, because the pain was unbearable, Marin dropped her head against the seat. The grayness got darker. Thicker. The pain just kept building. Throbbing. Consuming her.

And her son continued to cry.

That was the worst pain of all—her son crying.

Somehow she had to help him.

She tried to move again, to see his face, but her body no longer responded to what she was begging it to do. It was as if she were spiraling downward into a bottomless dark pit. Her breath was thin, her heartbeat barely a whisper in her ears. And her mouth was filled with the metallic taste of her own blood.

God, was she dying?

The thought broke her heart. She wasn't scared to die. But her death would leave her son vulnerable. Unprotected.

That couldn't happen.

"You can't let them take Noah," she heard herself whisper. She was desperate now, past desperate, and if necessary she would resort to begging.

"Who can't take him?" Lucky asked. He sounded so far away, but the warmth of his weight was still on her. She could feel his frantic breath gusting against her face.

"My parents." Marin wanted to explain that they were toxic people, that she didn't want them anywhere near her precious son. But there seemed so little breath left in her body, and she needed to tell him something far more important. "If I don't make it…"

"You will," he insisted.

Marin wasn't sure she believed that. "If I don't make it, get Noah out of here." She had to take a breath before she could continue. "Protect him." She coughed as she pulled the smoke and ash into her lungs. "Call Lizette Raines in Fort Worth. She'll know what to do."

Marin listened for a promise that he would do just that. And maybe Lucky Bacelli made that promise. Maybe he spoke to her, or maybe it was just her imagination when the softly murmured words filtered through the unbearable pain rifling in her head.

I swear, I'll protect him.

She wanted to see her son's face. She wanted to give him one last kiss.

But that didn't happen.

The grayness overtook her, and Marin felt her world fade to nothing.

Chapter Two

Working frantically, Lucky slung off the debris that was covering Marin Sheppard and her son.

No easy feat.

There was a lot of it, including some shards of glass and splintered metal, and he had to dig them out while trying to keep a firm grip on Noah. Not only was the baby screaming his head off, he wriggled and squirmed, obviously trying to get away from the nightmare.

Unfortunately, they were trapped right in the middle of it.

"You're okay, buddy," Lucky said to the baby. He hoped that was true.

Lucky quickly checked, but didn't see any obvious injuries. Heck, not even a scratch, which almost certainly qualified as a miracle.

As he'd seen Marin do, Lucky brushed a kiss on the boy's cheek to reassure him. Though it wasn't much help. Noah might have only been eight months old, but he no doubt knew something was horribly wrong.

This was no simple train derailment. An explosion.

An accident, maybe. Perhaps some faulty electrical component caused it. Or an act of terrorism.

The thought sickened him.

Whatever the cause, the explosion had caused a lot of damage. And a fire. Lucky could feel the flames and the heat eating their way toward them. There wasn't much time. A couple of minutes, maybe less.

And even then, getting out wasn't guaranteed.

They couldn't go through the window. There were jagged, thick chunks of glass still locked in place in the metal frame. It wouldn't be easy to kick out the remaining glass, and it'd cut them to shreds if he tried to go through it with Noah and Marin, especially since she was unconscious. Still, he might have to risk it. Lucky had no idea what he was going to face once he left the car and went into the hall toward the exit.

Maybe there was no exit left.

Maybe there was no other way out.

"Open your eyes, Marin," he said when he finally made it through the debris to her.

Oh, man.

There wasn't a drop of color in her face. And the blood. There was way too much of it, and it all seemed to be coming from a wound on the left side of her head. The blood had already seeped into her dark blond hair, staining one side of it crimson red.

"Look at me, Marin!" Lucky demanded.

She didn't respond.

Lucky shoved his fingers to her neck. It took him several snail-crawling moments to find her pulse. Weak but steady.

Thank God, she was alive.

For now.

But he didn't like the look of that gash on her head. Since she was breathing, there was no reason for him to do CPR, but he tried to revive her by gently tapping her face. It didn't work, and he knew he couldn't waste any more time.

Soon, very soon, the train would be engulfed in flames, and their chances of escape would be slim to none. They could be burned alive. He wasn't about to let that happen to her or the precious cargo in his arms. He'd made a promise to protect Noah, and that was a promise he intended to keep.

Moving Marin could make her injuries worse, but it was a risk he had to take. Placing Noah on her chest and stomach, he scooped them both up in his arms and hugged them tightly against him so that Noah wouldn't fall. Noah obviously wasn't pleased about that arrangement because he screamed even louder.

Lucky kicked aside a chunk of the displaced wall, and hurrying, he went through what was left of the doorway that divided the lounge car from the rest of the train. A blast of thick smoke shot right at him. He ducked his head down, held his breath and started running.

The hall through coach seating was an obstacle course. There was wreckage, smoke and at least a dozen other passengers also trying to escape. It was a stampede, and he was caught in the middle with Noah and Marin.

The crowd fought and shoved, all battering against

each other. All fighting to get toward the end of the car. And they finally made it. Lucky broke through the emergency exit and launched himself into the fresh air.

Landing hard and probably twisting his ankle in the process, he didn't stop. He knew all too well that there could be a secondary explosion, one even worse than the first, so he carried Noah and Marin to a clear patch about thirty yards from the train.

The November wind was bitter cold, but his lungs were burning from the exertion. So were the muscles in his arms and legs. He had to fight to hold on to his breath. The air held the sickening smell of things that were never meant to be burned.

He lay Marin and Noah down on the dried winter grass beside him, but Noah obviously intended to be with Lucky. He clamped his chubby little arms around Lucky's neck and held on, gripping him in a vise.

"You're okay," Lucky murmured. And because he didn't know what else to say, he repeated it.

To protect Noah from the wind and cold, Lucky tucked him inside his leather jacket and zipped it up as far as he could. Noah didn't protest. But he did look up at him, questioning him with tear-filled eyes. That look, those tears broke Lucky's heart. It was a look that would haunt him for the rest of his life.

"Your mom's going to be all right," Lucky whispered.

He prayed that was true.

Lucky pulled Marin closer so his body heat would keep her warm, and used his hand and shirt sleeve as a compress. He applied some gentle pressure against her injured head, hoping it would slow the bleeding. She didn't move when he touched her, not even a twitch.

He heard the first wail of ambulance sirens. Already close. Thankfully, they were just on the outskirts of Austin so the response time would be quick. The firefighters wouldn't be far behind. Lucky knew the drill. They'd set up a triage system, and the passengers with the most severe, but treatable injuries would be seen first. That meant Marin. She'd get the medical attention she needed.

"You're going to stay alive, Marin," Lucky ordered. "You hear me? Stay alive. The medics are on the way. Listen to the sirens. Listen! They're getting closer. They'll be here in just a few minutes."

Noah volleyed uncertain glances between Lucky and his mother. He stuck out his quivering bottom lip. For a moment Lucky thought the little boy might burst into tears again, but he didn't. Maybe the shock and adrenaline caught up with him, because even though his eyes watered, he stuck his thumb in his mouth and snuggled against Lucky.

It wasn't a sensation Lucky had counted on.

But it was a damn powerful one.

What was left of his breath vanished, and feelings went through him that he'd never experienced. Feelings he couldn't even identify except for the fact that they brought out every protective instinct in his body.

"What are your injuries?" Lucky heard someone shout. He looked up and saw a pair of medics racing toward him. They weren't alone. More were running toward some of the other passengers.

"We're not hurt. But she is," Lucky said pulling back his hand from Marin's injured head.

The younger of the two, a dark-haired woman, didn't take Lucky's word about not being injured. She began to examine Noah and him. Noah whined and tried to bat her hands away when she checked his pupils. The other medic, a fortysomething Hispanic man, went to work on Marin.

"She's Code Yellow," the medic barked to his partner. "Head trauma."

That started a flurry of activity, and the woman yelled for a stretcher.

Code Yellow. Marin's condition was urgent, but she was likely to survive.

"I need your name," the female medic insisted, forcing his attention back to her. "And the child's."

Lucky's stomach clenched.

It was a simple request. And it was standard operating procedure for triage processing. But Lucky knew it was only the beginning of lots of questions. If he answered some of those questions, especially the part about Noah being a near stranger, they'd take the little boy right out of his arms, and the authorities would hold on to him until they could contact the next of kin.

The very thing that Marin didn't want to happen.

Because her parents and her brother, Dexter, were Noah's next of kin.

Some choice.

As if he understood what was going on, Noah looked up at him with those big blue-green eyes. There were no questions. No doubts. Not even a whimper.

But there was trust. Complete, unconditional trust.

Noah's eyelids fluttered down, his thumb went back in his mouth, and he rested his cheek against Lucky's heart.

Oh, man.

It seemed like some symbolic gesture, but it probably had more to do with the kid's sheer exhaustion than anything else. Still, Lucky couldn't push it aside. Nor could he push aside what Marin had asked of him when they'd been trying to stay alive.

If I don't make it, get Noah out of here. Protect him.

And in that crazy life-or-death moment, Lucky had promised her that he would do just that.

It was a promise he'd keep.

"Sir," the medic prompted. "I need you to tell me the child's name."

It took Lucky a moment to say anything. "I'm Randall Davidson. This is my son, Noah," he lied. He tipped his head toward Marin. "And she's my fiancé, Marin Sheppard."

In order to protect the frightened little boy in his arms, Lucky figured he'd have to continue that particular lie for an hour or two until Marin regained consciousness or until he could call her friend in Fort Worth. Not long at all, considering his promise.

He owed Noah and Marin that much.

And he might owe them a hell of a lot more.

Chapter Three

Marin heard someone say her name.

It was a stranger's voice.

She wondered if it was real or all part of the relentless nightmare she'd been having. A nightmare of explosions and trains. At least, she thought it might be a train. The only clear image that kept going through her mind was of a pair of snakeskin boots. Everything else was a chaotic blur of sounds and smells and pain. Mostly pain. There were times when it was unbearable.

"Marin?" she heard the strange voice say again.

It was a woman. She sounded real, and Marin thought she might have felt someone gently touch her cheek.

She tried to open her eyes and failed the first time, but then tried again. She was instantly sorry that she'd succeeded. The bright overhead lights stabbed right into her eyes and made her wince.

Marin groaned.

Just like that, with a soft click, the lights went away. "Better?" the woman asked.

Marin managed a nod that hurt, as well.

The dimmed lighting helped, but her head was still throbbing, and it seemed as if she had way too many nerves in that particular part of her body. The pain was also affecting her vision. Everything was out of focus.

"Where am I?" Marin asked.

Since her words had no sound, she repeated them. It took her four tries to come up with a simple audible three-word question. Quite an accomplishment though, considering her throat was as dry as west Texas dust.

"St. Mary's," the woman provided.

Marin stared at her, her gaze moving from the woman's pinned-up auburn hair to her perky cotton-candy-pink uniform. Her name tag said she was Betty Garcia, RN. That realization caused Marin to glance around the room.

"I'm in a hospital?" Marin licked her lips. They were dry and chapped.

"Yes. You don't remember being brought here?"

Marin opened her mouth to answer, only to realize that she didn't have an answer. Until a few seconds ago, she'd thought she was having a nightmare. She definitely didn't remember being admitted to a hospital.

"Are you real?" Marin asked, just to make sure she wasn't trapped in the dream.

The woman smiled. "I'm going to assume that's not some sort of philosophical question. Yes, I'm real. And so are you." She checked the machine next to the bed. "How do you feel?"

Marin made a quick assessment. "I feel like someone bashed me in the head."

The woman made a sound of agreement. "Not someone. *Something*. But you're better now. You don't remember the train accident?"

"The accident," Marin repeated, trying to sort through the images in her head.

"It's still under investigation," the nurse continued. She touched Marin's arm. "But the authorities think there was some kind of electrical malfunction that caused the explosion."

An explosion. She remembered that.

Didn't she?

"Thankfully, no one was killed," the woman went on. She picked up Marin's wrist and took her pulse. "But over a dozen people were hurt, including you."

It was the word *hurt* that made the memories all come flooding back. The call from her grandmother, telling Marin that she was sick and begging her to come home. The train trip from Fort Worth to San Antonio.

The explosion.

God, the explosion.

"Noah!" Marin shouted. "Where's my son?"

Marin jackknifed to a sitting position, and she would have launched herself out of the bed if Nurse Garcia and the blinding pain hadn't stopped her.

"Easy now," the nurse murmured. She released her grip on Marin's wrist and caught on to her shoulders instead, easing her down onto the mattress.

Marin cooperated, but only because she had no choice. "My son—"

"Is fine. He wasn't hurt. He didn't even get a scratch."

The relief was as overwhelming as the pain. Noah

was all right. The explosion that had catapulted
through the air had obviously hurt her enough that she
needed to be hospitalized, but her son had escaped
unharmed.

Marin considered that a moment.

How had he escaped?

A clear image of Lucky Bacelli came into her head.

The man she'd been certain was following her. He'd
promised to get Noah out, and apparently he had.

"I want to see Noah," Marin insisted. "Could you
bring him to me now?"

Nurse Garcia stared at her, and the calm serenity
that had been in her coffee-colored eyes quickly faded
to concern. "Your son's not here."

Marin was sure there was some concern in her own
eyes, as well. "But—"

"Do you have any idea how long you've been in the
hospital?" the nurse interrupted.

Marin opened her mouth, closed it and considered
the question. She finally shook her head. "How long?"

"Nearly two days."

"Days?" Not hours. Marin was sure it'd only been a
few hours. Or maybe she was simply hoping it had
been. "So where is he? Who's had my baby all this
time?" But the moment she asked, the fear shot through
her. "Not my parents. Please don't tell me he's with
them."

A very unnerving silence followed, and Nurse
Garcia's forehead bunched up.

That did it.

Marin pushed aside the nurse's attempts to

her and tried to get out of the bed. It wasn't easy, nowhere close, but she fought through the pain and wooziness and forced herself to stand up.

She didn't stay vertical long.

Marin's legs turned boneless, and she had no choice but to slouch back down on the bed.

"There isn't any reason for you to worry," the nurse assured her. "Your son is okay."

Marin gasped for breath so she could speak. "Yes, so you've said. But who has him?"

"Your fiancé, of course. His father."

What breath she'd managed to regain, Marin instantly lost. "His…father?"

Nurse Garcia nodded, smiling. The bunched up forehead was history.

Marin experienced no such calmness. Adrenaline and fear hit her like a heavyweight's punch.

Noah's father was dead. He was killed in a boating accident nearly eight months before Noah was even born. There was no way he could be here.

"Your fiancé should be arriving any minute," the nurse cheerfully added.

Nothing could have kept Marin in the bed. Ignoring the nurse's protest and the weak muscles in her legs, Marin got up and went in search of her clothes. But even if she had to leave the hospital in her gown, she intended to get out of there and see what was going on.

Nurse Garcia caught on to her arm. Her expression changed, softened. "Everything's okay. There's no need for you to panic."

Oh, yes, there was. Either Randall had returned from the grave or something was terribly wrong. Noah had no father, and she had no fiancé.

There was a knock at the door. One soft rap before it opened. The jeans, the black leather jacket. The boots.

Lucky Bacelli.

Not Randall.

"Where's Noah?" she demanded.

Lucky ignored her question and strolled closer. "You gave me quite a scare, you know that? I'm glad you're finally awake." And with that totally irrelevant observation, he smiled. A secretive little smile that only he and Mona Lisa could have pulled off.

"I want to see Noah," Marin snapped. "And I want to see him now."

Another smile caused a dimple to wink in his left cheek. He reached out, touched her right arm and rubbed softly. A gesture no doubt meant to soothe her. It didn't work. For one thing, it was too intimate. Boy, was it. For another, nothing would soothe her except for holding her son and making sure he was okay.

"The doctor wants to examine you before he allows any other visitors so Noah's waiting at the nurses' station," Lucky explained, his voice a slow, easy drawl. The sound and ease of Texas practically danced off the words. "And I'm sure they're spoiling him rotten."

Marin disregarded the last half of his comment. Her son was at the nurses' station. That's all she needed to know. She ducked around Lucky and headed toward the door. Marin had no idea where the nurses' station was, but she'd find it.

Lucky stepped in front of her, blocking her path. "Where are you going, darling?"

That stopped her in her tracks.

Darling?

He said it as if he had a right to.

That was well past being intimate. Then he slid his arm around her waist and leaned in close. Too close. It violated her personal space and then some. Marin slapped her palm on his chest to stop him from violating it further.

"Is there a problem?" Nurse Garcia asked.

"You bet there is," Marin informed her.

And she would have voiced exactly what that problem was if she'd had the chance.

She hadn't.

Because in that same moment, Lucky Bacelli curved his hand around her waist and gently pulled her closer to him. He put his mouth right against her ear. "This was the only way," he whispered.

Marin tried to move away, but he held on. "The only way for what?" she demanded.

"To keep you and Noah safe." He kept his voice low, practically a murmur.

Even with the pain and fog in her head and his barely audible voice, she understood what he meant. Lucky had needed to protect Noah from her parents, just as she'd asked him to do. He'd pretended to be Randall Davidson, a dead man. Marin couldn't remember how Lucky had known Randall's name. Had she mentioned it? She must have. Thankfully, her parents had never met Randall and knew almost nothing about him. They certainly didn't know he was dead. She'd kept that from them because if she'd explained his death, she would have also had to endure countless questions about their life together.

Marin stopped struggling to get away from him and wearily dropped her head on his shoulder. He'd lied, but he'd done it all for Noah's sake. "My parents tried to take him?"

Lucky nodded. "They tried and failed. But I'm pretty sure they'll be back soon for round two."

That wasn't a surprise. With her in a hospital bed, her parents had probably thought they could take over her life before she even regained consciousness. It'd been a miracle that Lucky had been able to stop them, and if he'd had to do that with lies, then it was a small price to pay for her to be able to keep her son from them.

"Thank you," Marin mouthed.

"Don't thank me." Lucky moved back enough to allow their gazes to connect. The gray in his eyes turned stormy. "I don't think that train accident was really an accident," he whispered.

Stunned, Marin shook her head. "What do you mean?"

It seemed as if he changed his mind a dozen times about what to say. "Marin, Noah and you were nearly killed because of me."

Chapter Four

Lucky braced himself for the worst. A slap to the face. A shouted accusation. But Marin just stepped back and stared at him.

"What did you say?" she asked. Lucky wasn't sure how she managed to speak. The air swooshed out of her body, and the muscles in her jaw turned to steel.

Lucky didn't repeat his bombshell. Nor did he explain. He glanced over at the nurse. "Could you please give me a few minutes alone with my fiancée?"

Nurse Garcia nodded. "But only if Ms. Sheppard gets back in bed."

"Of course." Lucky caught on to Marin to lead her in that direction, but he encountered some resistance. Their eyes met, and in the depth of all that blue and green, he saw the debate going on. He also saw the moment she surrendered.

He knew she expected her cooperation to get her some fast answers. Unfortunately, Lucky didn't have any answers that she was going to like.

"You have five minutes. I don't want Ms. Sheppard

getting too tired," the nurse informed them. "I'll see if I can figure out a way to get Noah in here so you can have a quick kiss and cuddle."

"Thank you," Marin told the woman without taking her gaze from Lucky. She didn't say another word until the nurse was out of the room.

"Start talking," Marin insisted, her voice low and laced with a warning. "What do you mean you're responsible for nearly getting us killed? The nurse said it was an accident. Caused by an electrical malfunction."

That warning was the only thing lethal looking about her. She was pale and trembling. Lucky got her moving toward the bed. He also gave her gown an adjustment so that it actually covered her bare backside. Then, he got on with his explanation.

"The police first believed the explosion was caused by something electrical," Lucky explained. "But there are significant rumblings that when the Texas Rangers came in, they found an incendiary device."

But that was more than just rumblings. The sheriff had confirmed it.

Which brought him back to Marin's question.

"I'm a PI. And a former cop," he told her. With just those few crumbs of info, he had to pause and figure out how to say the rest. Best not to give Marin too much too soon. She was still weak. But he owed her at least part of the truth. "I've been working on a case that involves some criminals in hiding."

Well, one criminal in particular. That was a detail he'd keep to himself for now.

"I think someone associated with the case I'm investigating might have set that explosive," Lucky explained. "I believe there are people who don't want me to learn the truth about a woman who was murdered."

He waited for her reaction.

Marin paused, taking a deep breath. "I see."

Those two little words said a lot. They weren't an accusation. More like reluctant acceptance. He supposed that was good. It meant she might not slap him for endangering her son. Too bad. Lucky might have felt better if she *had* slapped him.

"The authorities know the explosion might be connected to you?" she asked.

"They know. The train was going through LaMesa Springs when the explosives went off. The sheriff there, Beck Tanner, is spearheading the initial investigation. He's already questioned me, and I told him about the case I was working on."

Sheriff Tanner would likely question Marin, too. Before that, Lucky would have to tell her the whole truth about why he was really on that train.

And the whole truth was guaranteed to make her slap him.

Or worse.

Marin looked down at her hands and brushed her fingers over her scraped knuckles. "The explosion wasn't your fault," she concluded. "You were just doing your job. And I put you in awkward position by asking you to protect Noah." She lifted her head. "I don't regret that. I can't."

Lucky pulled the chair next to her bed closer and sat down so they were at eye level. But they were still a safe distance from each other. Touching her was out. Her weakness and vulnerability clouded his mind.

And touching her would cloud his body.

He didn't need either.

"Yeah. After I met your parents, I totally understood why you asked me to take care of your little guy," Lucky continued. "Though at the time I thought I'd only have to keep that promise for an hour or two."

She nodded. "And then I didn't regain consciousness right away."

That was just the first of several complications.

"Like you asked, I tried getting in touch with your friend, Lizette Raines, in Fort Worth. She didn't answer her home phone, so I finally called someone I knew in the area and asked him to check on her. According to the neighbors, she's on a short trip to Mexico with her boyfriend."

Marin groaned softly. "Yes. She met him about two months ago, and I knew things were getting more serious, but she didn't mention anything about a trip."

She ran her fingers through the side of her shoulder-length hair and winced when she encountered the injury that had caused her concussion and the coma. In addition to the bandage that covered several stitches, her left temple was bruised—and the purplish stain bled all the way down to her cheekbone. It sickened him to see that on her face, to know what she'd been through.

And to know that it wasn't over.

This—whatever this was—was just beginning, and Lucky didn't care much for the bad turn it'd taken on that train.

"I wonder why Lizette didn't call me," Marin said. "She has my cell number."

"Your phone was lost in the explosion so even if she'd tried that number, she wouldn't have gotten you. Don't worry. Your friend's trip sounded legit, and none of your neighbors are concerned."

Before Lucky could continue, the door flew open, and a couple walked in. Not the nurse with Noah, but two people that Lucky had already met. And they were two people he had quickly learned to detest.

Marin's parents, Lois and Howard Sheppard.

The unexpected visit brought both him and Marin to their feet. It wasn't a fluid movement for Marin. She wobbled a bit when she got out of bed, and he slid his arm around her waist so she could keep her balance.

Lucky so wished he'd had time to prepare Marin for this. Of course, there was no preparation for the kind of backstabbing she was about to encounter.

"Mother," Marin said. Because she was pressed right against him, Lucky felt her muscles tense. She pulled in a long, tight breath.

No frills. That was the short physical description for the petite woman who strolled toward them. A simple maroon dress. Matching heels. Matching purse. Heck, even her lipstick matched. There wasn't a strand of her graying blond hair out of place. Lois Sheppard looked like the perfect TV mom.

She hurried toward Marin and practically elbowed Lucky out of the way so she could hug her daughter. When Lois pulled back, her eyes were shiny with tears.

"It's so good to see you, sweetheart," Lois said, her voice weepy and soft.

Marin stepped back out of her mother's embrace.

The simple gesture improved Lois's posture. "Marin, that's no way to act. Honestly, you'd think you have no manners. Aren't you even going to say hello to your father?"

"Hello," Marin echoed.

And judging from Marin's near growling tone, she didn't like her dad any better than Lucky did. Unlike Lois, Howard had a slick oily veneer that reminded Lucky of con artists and dishonest used car salesmen. Of course, his opinion probably had something to do with this whole backstabbing mission.

"Mother, why are you and Dad here?"

Lois shrugged as if the answer were obvious. "Because we love you. Because we're concerned about you. You're coming back to the ranch with us so you can have time to recuperate from your injuries. You know you're not well enough or strong enough to be on your own. You never have been. Clearly, leaving home was a mistake."

Lucky pulled Marin tighter into the crook of his arm.

"I'm not going with you," she informed her mother.

Lucky wanted to cheer her backbone, but he already knew the outcome of this little encounter.

There'd be no cheering today.

"Yes, you are," Lois disagreed. "I'm sorry, but I can't give you a choice about that. You and Noah are too important to us. And because we love you both so much, we've filed papers."

Lucky felt Marin's muscles stiffen even more. "What kind of papers?" Marin enunciated each syllable.

Lucky didn't wait for Lois Sheppard to provide the explanation. "Your folks are trying to use your hospital stay and your epilepsy to get custody of Noah." He turned his attention to Lois and made sure he smirked. "Guess what—not gonna happen."

The woman's maroon-red mouth tightened into a temporary bud. "I don't think you'll have much of a say in that, Randall."

"Lucky," he corrected. Because by damn he might have to play the part of Marin's slimeball ex, but Lucky refused to use the man's name. It'd been a godsend that neither of Marin's parents had ever met said slimeball. If they had, the charade of Lucky pretending to be him would have been over before it even started.

"I don't care what you call yourself," Howard interceded. "You're an unfit father. You weren't even there for the birth of your own son. You left Marin alone to fend for herself."

Lucky shoved his thumb to his chest. "Well, I'm here now."

"Are you?" Howard challenged.

"What the hell does that mean?" Lucky challenged right back.

Howard didn't answer right away, and the silence intensified with his glare. "It means I don't think you love my daughter. I think this so-called relationship between you two is a sham to convince Lois and me that we don't need to intervene in Marin's life."

Since that was the truth, Lucky knew it was time for

some damage control. Later, he'd figure out if Howard really knew something or if this was a bluff.

Lucky pulled Marin closer to him. Body against body. Marin must have felt the same need for damage control because she came up on her toes and kissed him, a familiar peck of reassurance. Something a real couple would have shared.

That brief lip-lock speared through him, causing Lucky to remind himself that this really was a sham.

"What papers have they filed?" Marin asked him.

Lucky didn't take his gaze from Howard. "Your parents convinced a judge to review your competency as a parent. A crooked judge is my guess, because we have to go to your parents' ranch for an interview with a psychologist."

Lucky expected Marin to lose it then and there. Maybe a tirade or some profanity. He wouldn't have blamed her if she had. But her reaction was almost completely void of emotion.

"Mother, Dad, you're leaving now," Marin said. And she stepped out of Lucky's arms and sat back down on the bed. A moment passed before she looked at her mother again. "I'm tired. I need my rest. Nurse's orders."

Lois took a step closer, and even though she wasn't smiling, there was a certain victory shout in her stance. "If you don't return to the ranch and do this interview with the psychologist, the judge will intervene. Noah will be taken from you and placed in our custody."

And with that threat, Lois and Howard finally did what Marin had asked. They turned and walked out the door.

All that cool and calmness that Marin had displayed went south in a hurry. She began to shake, and for a moment Lucky thought she might be going into shock or on the verge of having a seizure.

Instead, she wrapped her arms around herself. "What do I have to do to make this go away?"

Since there was no easy way to put it, Lucky just laid it out there for her. "We'll have to go to the ranch because as your legal next of kin, your parents managed to get an emergency hearing in front of a judge who's also their friend. They persuaded this judge that you need to be medically monitored—by them, under their roof. And the judge signed a temporary order. Once we're at the ranch, we'll have the interview where we'll need to convince a psychologist that we're a happy couple fit to raise Noah. If we do that, the psychologist will pass that on to the judge, and there won't be another hearing. The temporary order will expire, and you'll keep sole custody of Noah."

Marin slowly lifted her eyes and looked at him. She didn't exactly voice a question, but there were plenty of nonverbal ones.

"The interview could be as early as tomorrow afternoon," Lucky added. "If the doctor releases you from the hospital today. That means we wouldn't have to keep up the charade for long. Then, after visiting with your grandmother, you can go home."

Well, maybe.

That was one of those gray areas that Lucky hadn't quite figured out. Marin might never be able go home. It might not be safe.

"And what happens if we come clean and tell everyone that you're not Noah's father?" she asked. But Marin immediately waved that off. "Then my parents will use that against me. They might even want a paternity test. They'll brand us as liars. And if the judge knows we lied about that, he'll assume we're lying about my ability to be a good parent."

The Sheppards might even try to file criminal charges against him for preventing them from taking Noah. The couple certainly had a lot of misplaced love, and they were aiming all of it at Marin and Noah.

"I'll fight it," Marin said, sounding not nearly as strong as her words. "I'll hire a lawyer and fight it."

"I've already talked to one," he assured her. "I called a friend of a friend, and she says to cooperate for now. Your mother and Howard might have this judge firmly in their pockets, and he's the one who arranged for the interview with the psychologist. I've requested a change of venue, and he denied it. The only way we could have gotten a delay is if you hadn't come out of the coma."

"Great. Just great." She paused a moment. "So you're saying we should go to the ranch and do as my parents say?"

"I don't think we have a choice."

Her chin came up. "Yes, I do. There's no reason to drag you into this. And you shouldn't have to be subjected to staying with my parents. You have no idea the emotional hell they'll put you through, especially since they believe we're a couple. A couple they want to see driven apart."

Lucky didn't doubt that. But there was another

problem. "Marin, your parents aren't going to just give up. It took some fast talking for me to stop an immediate transfer of custody. Your mother was here early yesterday morning. She came prepared to take Noah then and there."

Marin groaned and buried her face in her hands. "Oh, God."

Lucky groaned right along with her. There were a lot of things wrong with their plan. For one thing, it wasn't legal. But what Marin's parents were trying to do wasn't right, either. So maybe two wrongs did make a right.

That still didn't mean this would be easy.

For two days, he'd have to pretend to be Noah's father and Marin's loving fiancé. The first was a piece of cake. It was that second one that was giving him the most trouble.

Lucky blamed it on the blazing attraction between them.

Before he'd held Marin in his arms, before that brief kiss, he'd only lusted after her in his heart. Now, he was lusting after her in all kinds of ways. And he couldn't do anything about it.

Because Marin might become a critical witness when he busted his investigation wide open. She might be the key to finally getting justice. He couldn't compromise that—it was the most important thing in his life.

He couldn't get involved with Marin. He could only live a temporary lie.

"Okay," Marin mumbled. She cleared her throat. "So, you have to do the interview, whenever that'll be, but you don't have to stay at the ranch in Willow Ridge. You can drop Noah and me off and then say you have an urgent business appointment or something, that you'll return in time for the interview."

Lucky just stared at her, wondering how she was going to handle what he had to say.

"You're already having second thoughts?" Marin concluded.

"No. That interview has to happen. You have to keep custody of Noah."

Now it was Marin's turn to stay silent for several moments. "And you'd do this for me?" Marin asked. Her gaze met his again, and there was no cowering look in her eyes. Just some steel and attitude. "Why?"

She wasn't requesting information. She was demanding it.

This would have been a good time to tell another half truth. Especially since—much to his disgust—he was getting good at them.

But another lie would stick in his throat.

"I'm looking for your brother, Dexter," he confessed.

Her eyes immediately darkened, and he saw the pulse pound on her throat. "You followed me on the train?"

Lucky nodded. "I followed you."

"Why?" she repeated, though this one had even more steel than the original one.

"Because I thought you might lead me to him."

She tipped her eyes to the ceiling and groaned. "I was right about you. You're one of those men. The ones who've followed me and tried to scare me."

He reached out to her, but Marin batted his hands away. "Scaring you was never my intention. I just need to find your brother."

"What do you want from Dexter?" she snapped.

Lucky was betting this answer wasn't so obvious. "The truth?"

She sliced at him with a scalpel-sharp glare. "That would be nice for a change."

He debated if Marin was strong enough to hear this. Probably not. But there was no turning back now. He toyed with how he should say it. But there was only one way to deliver news like this. Quick and dirty.

He'd tell her the truth even if it made Marin hate him.

Chapter Five

Marin stared at Lucky, holding her breath.

Even though she'd only known him for a short period of time, she was already familiar with his body language.

Whatever he had to say wouldn't be good.

"What do you want from my brother?" she repeated.

Lucky stood and looked down at her. He met her gaze head-on. "I want him dead."

Everything inside her stilled. It wasn't difficult to process that frightening remark since she'd been through this before. For the past year, she'd had to deal with other men who had wanted to find Dexter, too. And like Lucky they probably had wanted him dead, as well. But this cut even deeper to the bone because Lucky had saved her son. He'd saved her.

And she trusted him.

Correction, she *had* trusted him. Right now, she just felt betrayed.

Marin tried to keep her voice and body calm, which was hard to do with her emotions in shreds. She silently cursed the pain that pounded through her head and made it hard to think. "Then, you already have what you want. Dexter *is* dead."

Lucky lifted his left shoulder. "I'm not so sure about that."

The other men hadn't been sure, either. But then neither had her own family. "If Dexter were alive, he would have contacted me by now. He wouldn't have let me believe he was dead."

At least she hoped that was true. But Marin couldn't be certain, especially considering the dangerous circumstances surrounding his disappearance.

"Let's just say that I know a different side of your brother," Lucky insisted. "The man I know would do anything—and I mean anything—to save himself. And in this case, making everyone think he's dead is about the only thing that could save him from the investors who poured millions of dollars into research that didn't pay off for them because Dexter didn't deliver what he promised he would."

She couldn't disagree with that. Marin had examined and reexamined every detail she could find about the night Dexter had disappeared.

Lucky had no doubt done the same.

"What do you know about the night my brother died?" she asked.

His eyes said "too much." "Your brother was a chemical engineer working on a privately funded project. He was supposed to be testing antidotes for chemical agents, specifically a hybrid nerve agent that might be used in a combat situation against ground troops. The investors believed they could sell this antidote to the Department of Defense for a large sum of money. But something went wrong. The Justice Department got some info that Dexter was selling secrets, and they were about to launch a full-scale investigation."

Yes, she knew all of that—after the fact. Before that night, however, Marin hadn't known exactly what Dexter's research project entailed. Even now, she doubted that she knew the entire truth. Maybe no one did. But something had indeed gone wrong with the project, and the Justice Department investigation hadn't happened as planned because there had been an explosion in the research facility.

There was also evidence of some kind of attack that night, and a security guard who was actually an undercover Justice Department agent had been killed. The body had been found in the rubble of the facility.

Unlike Dexter's.

No one had been able to locate his body or those of the two women who'd been in the facility that night. But Marin believed Dexter had indeed been killed in the attack, which might have been orchestrated by someone who wanted to get their hands on her brother's research project.

Since the project was missing, as well, Marin was convinced that the culprit had succeeded.

"Your brother is a criminal," Lucky informed her.

Even though she was in pain and exhausted, Lucky's words gave her a boost of anger and adrenaline that she needed. But then, defending her brother had always been a strong knee-jerk reaction.

"There were never any charges brought against Dexter," Marin reminded him.

"Because the authorities think he's dead."

"No. Because there's no evidence to indicate he's done anything wrong."

"There's evidence," Lucky insisted. "I just haven't found it. Yet. But before his disappearance, Dexter was working on more than a chemical antidote. A chemical weapon. He was playing both sides of the fence, and three days ago a key component of that weapon surfaced for sale on the black market."

Now, that she didn't know. But perhaps her parents did. According to the phone conversations she'd had with her grandmother, the federal authorities had kept her parents informed about the investigation, and they'd visited the ranch often.

"That's still not proof Dexter's alive," Marin insisted, certain that her voice no longer sounded so convinced of Dexter's innocence.

Lucky lifted his hands, palms up. "Who else would be trying to sell that component?"

"The person who stole it."

He didn't toss his hands in the air again, but he looked as if he wanted to do just that. "Other than some blood found at the scene, there's no proof that Dexter is dead. *None.* He would have hung on to that weapon and waited until the right time to sell it. Three days ago was apparently the right time for him because it appeared."

Marin took a moment to rein in her emotions. Despite his sometimes selfish behavior, she loved her brother and didn't want to believe he was capable of doing something like this. She'd grieved for him, and she missed him. Would Dexter have put the family and her through all that pain just to cover himself?

Maybe.

And if so, then maybe Lucky was telling the truth. "Assuming you're right, then what does this case have to do with you?"

"Dexter pissed off the wrong people, Marin," Lucky explained. "And I'm one of those people."

That didn't sound like something a PI would say about one of his cases. It sounded personal. "What do you mean?"

His jaw muscles stirred. He eased back down into the chair and scrubbed his hands over his face. "My sister was fresh out of her doctoral program at the University of Texas, and her first and only real job was working for Dexter."

Marin sucked in her breath. This was starting to move in a direction that she didn't want to go. "Not Brenna Martel?" Brenna had been a colleague, one of the women who went missing and was presumed dead. But Brenna hadn't just been Dexter's business associate. She'd been his lover.

"No. Not Brenna. His lab assistant, Kinley Ford." He waited a moment. "My dad died right after Kinley was born, my mom remarried shortly thereafter, and Kinley took our stepdad's surname."

That's why Marin hadn't immediately made the connection between Lucky and the woman. She hadn't met Kinley Ford, but since her brother's disappearance, she had seen a photo of the young chemical engineer who'd assisted Dexter on his last project.

Kinley Ford had her brother's eyes.

And those storm-gray eyes were drilling into her, waiting for her to answer.

"The police believe your sister was killed that night," Marin whispered. "And unlike Dexter, there's evidence to point to that."

He nodded. And swallowed hard. "The cops think Brenna was killed, too. They found blood from all three of them. Just a trace from Dexter. More than a pint from Brenna. Triple that from my sister. There's no way she could have lived with that much blood loss."

"But the police didn't find the bodies of either woman," she pointed out.

Lucky shrugged. "Dexter probably hid them somewhere before he gave up and set the explosives to blow up the research lab. There was evidence that someone had tried to clean up the crime scene."

Yes, she'd read that, as well, and along with the fact that there'd been no lethal quantities of her brother's blood found, she could understand why some people believed he was still alive.

And guilty.

Though Lucky hadn't convinced her that Dexter was alive, he had convinced her of something—the pain he was feeling over the loss of his sister. She understood that loss because she'd grieved for Dexter. "I'm sorry Kinley was killed."

"Yeah. So am I." She heard the pain. It was raw and

still so close to the surface that she could practically feel it. "Your brother murdered her."

Marin didn't want to believe that, either. But she couldn't totally dismiss it. However, if Dexter was responsible, then it must have been an accident.

"You followed me because you thought I'd lead you to Dexter," she concluded.

He nodded. "I've been monitoring you for months. When I learned you were going to the ranch to see your grandmother, I figured Dexter would do the same."

A chill went through her. "You've been *monitoring* me? What the heck does that mean?"

He didn't get a chance to answer.

There was a tap at the door a split second before it opened. Marin didn't want the interruption. She wanted to finish this conversation with Lucky. But then, she saw that it wasn't her parents returning for round two. It was Nurse Garcia, and she had Noah in her arms.

The anger and frustration didn't exactly evaporate, but Marin did push aside those particular emotions along with her questions so that she could stand and go to her son. Just seeing him flooded her heart with love.

"Stay put. I'll bring this little guy to you," Nurse Garcia insisted. "I told the doctor you were awake and anxious for this visit. He was going to be tied up with another patient for an hour or so, but he agreed to let you see your son before the examination."

Noah smiled when he spotted Marin, and he began to pump his arms and legs. He babbled some excited indistinguishable sounds. Marin reached for him, and he went right into her arms. Nurse Garcia excused herself and left.

Marin didn't even try to blink her tears away. It was a miracle that she was holding her son, and an even greater miracle that he hadn't been hurt.

Noah tolerated the embrace for several seconds before he got bored. He leaned back and reached for the bandage on her head. Marin shifted him in her arms, and her son's attention landed on Lucky.

Noah immediately reached for him.

Her son had given her a warm reception, but it was mild compared to the one he gave Lucky. Noah squealed with delight and laughed when Lucky stood to give him a kiss on the cheek.

"I told you that your mom was okay, buddy," Lucky said to Noah.

When Noah's reach got more insistent and he began to fuss, Marin handed her son over to a man who was feeling more and more like her enemy.

"Sorry about that," Lucky mumbled, gathering Noah in his arms. "I've hardly let him out of my sight since the explosion. I guess he's gotten used to me."

"I guess." And she didn't bother to sound pleased about it.

"I wasn't sure what to feed him so I called a doctor friend and got some suggestions for formula and food. He said to go with rice cereal. I hope that was okay."

"Fine," she managed to say. "I guess you didn't have any trouble getting him to sleep?"

"Not really. But he's got a good set of lungs on him when he wants a bottle. Don't you, buddy?" Lucky grinned at Noah, the expression making him a little more endearing than she wanted at the moment.

Marin watched as Noah playfully batted at Lucky. Her son was at ease in this man's arms. More than at ease. The two looked like father and son. And they weren't. Lucky was simply a temporary stand-in.

Now, it was time to deal with reality.

The replacement father act had to be over soon, because she and Lucky obviously weren't on the same path. He not only hated her brother, he wanted revenge for his sister's death, and he'd been willing to use her to get to Dexter.

"Earlier you said you'd monitored me," she reminded him. "How?"

His grin evaporated, and even though he kept his attention on Noah, his expression became somber. "I rented the condo connected to yours."

The chill inside her got significantly colder. "You watched me? You listened in on my conversations?"

He nodded. "The walls between the condos are thin. It's not hard to overhear, if you're listening. And I was. I wanted to know if you were in contact with Dexter."

She silently cursed. "So you know I didn't. Still, you invaded my privacy."

"I did," Lucky readily admitted. "Because I had to do it. Whether you want to believe it or not, your brother's a dangerous man."

Marin groaned softly, looked at her son and blinked back more tears. "First, you save my son. You save me. And then you tell me that you've not only been spying on me, you want to kill my brother if by some miracle he's still alive."

"I don't want to kill him. I want him arrested so he can stand trial, be convicted and then get the death penalty."

"Oh, is that all?" The sarcasm dripped from her voice.

With Noah still gripped lovingly in his arms, Lucky stood back up. There was emotion in his eyes. But even though she owed this man a lot, she had just as much reason to despise him.

Marin hoped like the devil that she was keeping her temper in check because of her headache and Noah. Not because she was feeling anything like attraction for Lucky Bacelli.

But just looking at him gave her a little tug deep within her belly. She didn't want that tug to mean anything. She wanted it to go away. It was a primal reminder that no matter what he wanted from her brother, she was still hotly attracted to him.

"I'm not the only person after Dexter," Lucky continued. "Have you met Grady Duran?"

Oh, yes. And unlike what she was feeling for Lucky, there was no ambivalence when it came to Duran. She loathed Duran as much as she was afraid of him. Judging from their brief, heated encounters he thought she was a liar.

"Duran and my brother were in business together on the chemical antidote project. He believes Dexter is alive," she supplied. "For the past year he's been harassing me because he thinks I know more than I'm saying. The man's a bully, and he's dangerous."

"Did Duran hurt you?" Lucky immediately asked.

Marin's gaze rifled to his. Lucky's tone set off all sorts of alarms. That sounded like the tone of a man who was concerned.

About *her.*

Marin rethought that when she studied the ease he seemed to have when interacting with Noah. Maybe the alarm wasn't for her but for her son. That led her to another question.

Was there reason for concern?

"Duran didn't physically hurt me," Marin explained. "But he's one of the reasons I've tried to keep where I live secret. I was in Dallas for a while, but when he showed up, I moved to Fort Worth. The man frightens me because his desperation seems almost as intense as his determination to find Dexter."

Lucky's mouth tightened. "Duran probably knows about the chemical weapon's components surfacing on the black market. He might try to contact you again."

He paused, took a step toward her, halving the distance between them. "Marin, you have a lot to deal with, and you're not a hundred percent. Right now, just concentrate on recovering and getting through the interview that your parents set up."

Marin wanted to argue, but he was right. She also wanted to turn down Lucky's offer to pose as Noah's father. But she couldn't do that, either. She couldn't let her anger and pride cause her to lose custody. However, there was something she could do.

Something to put some distance between her and Lucky.

"All right," Marin agreed. "I'll check with the doctor and see how soon I can be discharged. Then, once he gives me the okay, I'll call a cab to take Noah and me to the ranch. When I know the exact time and place of the interview, I'll phone you and you can meet me at the psychologist's office. If all goes well, maybe it won't take more than an hour or two."

Lucky pulled in a deep breath and eased down on the bed beside her. The mattress creaked softly. "I should be at the ranch with you."

"No." Marin didn't even have to think about that— the tug in her belly had convinced her of that. "My parents will be expecting us to be a loving couple. In fact, they won't just be expecting it, they'll be looking for anything they can use against me to force me to return home for good."

"You need me there with you," he insisted.

She met his stare. The tug got worse. So, Marin dodged those lethal gray eyes. "I don't want to be coddled."

"Good." He leaned in, so close that it forced her to make eye contact again. "Because I'm not the coddling type."

No. He wasn't. There was a dangerous edge about him, and despite the gentleness he was showing her son, Marin didn't think this was his normal way of dealing with things. Lucky Bacelli was a lifetime bad boy.

The tug became a full-fledged pull.

Marin drew back. She had to. Because there was no

room in her life for a man, especially this man who could make her feel things she didn't want to feel.

He inched even closer. "Marin, I'm not giving you a choice about this. I'm coming to the ranch with Noah and you."

His adamancy didn't sit well with her. Especially after all the things he'd just admitted.

Then, it hit her.

She finally got why Lucky was so adamant. "You think Dexter had something to do with that explosion on the train?"

He gave a crisp nod. "Who else?"

"Not Dexter. My brother wouldn't hurt me," she informed him.

"If not him, then someone who was trying to stop me from getting to him. And that person didn't care if you or Noah got hurt in the process."

Lucky snared her gaze. "Marin, what I'm saying is that Noah and you could still be in serious danger."

Chapter Six

Lucky caught on to Marin's arm to help steady her as she walked through the door of her old room at her parents' ranch. But Marin would have no part of accepting his help. With Noah clutched in her arms, she moved out of Lucky's grip and tossed him a warning glance.

He tossed her one of his own.

"We aren't going to pull this off if you're shooting daggers at me," he mumbled.

She'd been giving him the silent treatment since they left the hospital an hour earlier. And because Noah had hardly made a peep the entire trip to the ranch, it'd been a very quiet drive in the rental car she'd arranged so that they wouldn't be in the same vehicle with her parents.

Lucky wasn't sure what to say to her anyway. Truth was, he had let her down. He'd gone onto that train to follow her, and even though he'd gotten Noah and her out of the burning debris, that wasn't going to negate one simple fact.

Marin didn't trust him.

Heck, she didn't even like him.

And that would make these next forty-eight hours damn uncomfortable.

His opinion about that didn't change when he glanced around the room. There were plenty of signs of Marin's life here. Her earlier life, that is, when she was still her parents' daughter. Several framed pictures of her sat on the dresser. In one she wore a pale pink promlike dress; in another, a dark blue graduation gown. But the photo in the middle, the one most prominently displayed was a shot of her standing between her parents. It was the most recent of the photographs, probably taken just shortly before her move to Dallas–Fort Worth.

She looked miserable.

"I figured all of this stuff would have been put in storage," Marin grumbled. "Instead, they've made it a sort of shrine."

They had indeed.

From the background investigation Lucky had run on her, Marin had left Willow Ridge in a hurry after a bitter argument with her parents over her relationship with Randall, the jerk her parents had thankfully never met. Before that, she'd lived and worked just a few miles away, running her CPA business from an office on Main Street in Willow Ridge. Her apartment had been over her office, and according to a former town resident that Lucky had interviewed, Marin's parents had visited her every day.

Marin had then met Randall while on a short business trip to New Orleans. The problems with her parents had started when Marin began dating him and had refused to bring him home so they could meet him. Maybe she'd done that because subconsciously she hadn't trusted Randall, but it probably had more to do with the fact that her parents had disapproved of all of her previous relationships.

This fake one would be no different.

"Obviously, we can't ask for separate rooms," Marin grumbled.

She was right about that. But at least the suite was big, thank goodness. Probably at least four hundred square feet, with a bathroom on one side. On the other there was a sitting room that had been converted to a nursery—complete with a crib and changing table.

There was only one bed though, covered with a garnet-red comforter.

Lucky followed the direction of Marin's gaze—the bed had obviously caught her attention, as well.

"Only two days," he reminded her.

Her heavy sigh reminded him that those two days would seem like an eternity. It was also a reminder that he should at least try to do some damage control because Lucky was positive that things could get a lot worse than they already were.

Lucky took off his leather jacket and placed it over the back of a chair that was perched in front of an antique desk. He adjusted the compact-size handgun that he had tucked in a slide holster at the back of his jeans.

Marin's gaze went racing to his holster. "Is that a gun?" she asked.

"Yes. I always carry it. I'm a PI, remember?"

She opened her mouth, closed it and turned away.

Great. Now, they had another issue. "We have to talk," Lucky insisted.

Another sigh. Marin sank down onto the edge of the bed and lay Noah next to her. The little boy didn't stay put, however. He rolled onto his stomach and tried to crawl away, but Marin caught on to him. Soon the tiny floral pattern in the comforter caught his eye, and Noah stopped crawling and began to pick at the embroidery.

"There really isn't anything to talk about," Marin countered. "I think you've made everything perfectly clear."

But then, her gaze came to his again. Lucky didn't exactly see a carte blanche acceptance there, but he did see and feel a slight change in her. She probably knew her animosity, though warranted, wasn't going to do them any good.

"You really think Noah and I are still in danger?" she asked.

He considered his answer. "Yes. And if I could do anything to change that, I would."

She wearily pushed her hair away from her bandaged forehead. "So would I. I even thought if I distanced myself from you that the danger would go away." Marin waved him off when Lucky started to respond to that. "But if the danger is connected to Dexter and the people who might want him and that chemical weapon, then no matter where I am, the danger will find me."

Marin stared at him. "How do I stop the danger from finding Noah?"

Since this wasn't going to be an easy answer, Lucky sat down beside her. "I won't let anything happen to Noah, understand?"

She shook her head. Then, swallowed hard. "I can't lose him."

"I know." And because he truly understood her concern and fear, Lucky reached out and slid his arm around her.

Marin stiffened, and for a moment he thought she might push him away. She didn't. But she didn't exactly melt into his arms, either. Still, this contact was better than the silent treatment.

Wasn't it?

Lucky rethought that when she looked at him. Just like that, he felt the hard punch of attraction. A punch he'd been trying to ward off since the first time he'd watched Marin with his surveillance equipment. Of course, he hadn't spoken to her then. At that time, he'd merely thought of her as Dexter Sheppard's sister who might have been hiding her brother's whereabouts. But she was more than that now.

And that wasn't good.

Lucky couldn't lose focus. He owed it to Kinley to find her killer, and he owed it to Noah to keep him safe. He couldn't do either if he was daydreaming about having sex with Marin.

But that little reminder didn't really help.

Next to him, Marin was warm, soft, and her scent was stirring things in him that were best left alone.

"On the train, you said you were hitting on me," she

commented, her voice practically a whisper as if discussing a secret. "Why did you lie about that?"

Now, that riled him. "Who said I lied?"

"You were following me to find Dexter."

"And I was hitting on you. Despite what you think of me, I can do two things at once."

She frowned and glanced down at the close contact. "Is that what you're doing now—hitting on me?" And it wasn't exactly an invitation to continue.

The knock at the door stopped anything stupid he was about to say. Or do. Like kiss her blind just to prove the attraction that was already way too obvious.

"It's me," the visitor called out.

"My grandmother," Marin provided, and she got up to open the door.

The petite woman who gave Marin a long hug was an older version of Lois, Marin's mother. Except unlike Lois, this woman had some warmth about her. Of course, Marin had come all this way to see her, so obviously there wasn't the tension she had with her parents.

Lucky got to his feet, as well, though he didn't move far from the bed in case Noah crawled closer to the edge.

"I'm Helen," the woman said, introducing herself to Lucky. Her dusty-blue eyes were as easy as her smile. "Welcome to Willow Ridge."

Her eye contact was hospitable, unlike the frostiness he'd gotten from Marin's parents when they'd arrived minutes earlier. Helen's scrutiny lasted only a few seconds though before the woman's attention landed on Noah. She smiled again. No. She *beamed* and went to the bed to sit next to her great-grandson.

"My, my, now aren't you a handsome-looking young man," Helen concluded. Noah stared at her a moment before he returned the smile. That caused Helen to giggle with delight, and she scooped up the little boy in her arms. "Why don't we go out on the patio and have a little visit."

Lucky was about to question whether Marin was up to going outside, but she followed her grandmother to a pair of French doors that thankfully led to a glass enclosed patio. No sting of the winter wind here. It was warm, cozy and had an incredible view of the west pasture that was green with winter rye grass. With the sun just starting to set, the room was filled with golden light.

"How are you feeling?" Helen asked, her attention going back to Marin. The older woman dropped down into one of the white wicker chairs.

"I'm fine," Marin assured her, taking the love seat next to her grandmother and son.

Everyone in that sunroom knew that was a lie. The dark smudgy circles beneath Marin's eyes revealed her draining fatigue. And then there was that bandage on her forehead, a stark reminder of how close she'd come to being killed. It would take Lucky a lifetime or two to forgive himself for not being able to stop what had happened.

"How are you feeling?" Marin countered.

Helen gave her a short-lived smile and showered

Noah's cheeks with kisses. "I figured the only way to get you here was to tell you I was under the weather."

Marin mumbled something under her breath. Then, huffed. "When you called Lizette earlier this week and asked her to give me a message, you said you were sick, not under the weather. *Sick.* I was worried about you."

"I know, and considering what happened on the train, I'm sorry. But I'm not sorry you're here." Helen paused a moment. "All of these problems with your folks need to be worked out, and this was the only way I could think to do it."

"Grandma, it didn't resolve anything. Mom and Dad are trying to take Noah from me."

"I know, and I'm sorry about that, too. I did try to stop them, but you know how your mother is when she gets an idea in her head." The smile returned. "But they'll forget all about custody and such when Dexter comes home."

That grabbed Lucky's complete attention. "You think Dexter's alive?"

"Of course. And he won't miss the chance to see his sister and nephew. I figure Dexter's been waiting for the best time to make his homecoming, and that time is now."

Lucky was about to agree, but Helen continued before he could speak. "I don't guess you'll be joining the family for dinner tonight?"

"No," Marin immediately answered. "Mom and Dad might have blackmailed me into staying here, but there's nothing in that judge's order that says I have to socialize with the people trying to take my son."

"I thought you'd feel that way. I'll make sure the cook brings in some trays for you two and some baby goodies for our little man here." Helen tipped her head toward the bedroom. "It's my guess that your folks have your suite bugged."

Lucky and Marin just stared at her.

Helen continued, "I heard them talking when they got back from the hospital after they saw you. Don't know where the bug is, but I'll bet my favorite broach that they put one somewhere in the bedroom."

"Why would they do that?" Lucky asked.

"Because they're suspicious. I don't know where Howard got the notion, but he thinks Lucky here is only out to break your heart. My advice, be careful what you say. And be just as careful what you do. Don't give Howard and Lois any ammunition to take this little boy. Because with a judge who's your dad's fishing buddy, they already have enough."

Marin groaned softly and started to get up. "I'll look for the bug."

Lucky put his hand on her shoulder and eased her back down. "I'll do it."

"You might not want to do that," Helen volunteered. "I mean, you could think of a bug as a golden opportunity to give Howard and my often misguided daughter a dose of their own medicine. After all, they're using deceit to try to force Marin back here. Why don't you prove to them that you have nothing to hide, that you are what you say you are?"

Lucky could think of a reason—because it would be damn impossible to stay "in character" 24/7. He would have to disarm that eavesdropping device.

His cell phone rang. He considered letting it go to voice mail. Until he spotted the name on the caller ID.

"I have to take this," he told Marin, and since he couldn't go into the bugged bedroom, he stepped outside so he could have some privacy.

Winter came right at him. The wind felt like razor blades whipping at his shirt and jeans. But that didn't stop him. This call was exactly what he'd been waiting for.

"Cal," Lucky answered. As in Special Agent Cal Rico from the Justice Department. Just as important, Cal was his best friend and had been since they'd grown up together in San Antonio. "Please tell me you have good news about that train explosion."

"Some." But Cal immediately paused. "It looks as though someone left a homemade explosive device in a suitcase in one of the storage lockers near the lounge car."

The car where they'd been sitting.

"I don't suppose you saw anyone suspicious carrying a black leather suitcase?" Cal asked.

"No." But then, Lucky had been preoccupied with Marin. He'd allowed the attraction he felt for her to stop him from doing his job. And his job had been to make sure that no one had followed him while he'd been following Marin.

Obviously, he'd failed big-time.

"Did any of the other passengers notice the suitcase-carrying bomber?" Lucky leaned his shoulder against the sunroom glass, hoping he'd absorb some of the heat. Inside, Marin and her grandmother were still talking.

"No, but I'm about to start reviewing the surveillance disks."

That caught Lucky's attention. "What exactly was recorded?"

"All the main areas on the train itself, and the two depots where the train stopped in Fort Worth and then in Dallas."

Good. It was what he wanted to hear. "So anyone who boarded should be on that surveillance?"

"Should be. Of course, that doesn't rule out a person who was already on the train. The person could have been hiding there for a while just so they wouldn't be so obvious on surveillance."

Hell. But Lucky would take what he could get. These disks were a start.

"We'll scan the disks using the face recognition program," Cal continued. "And also check for anyone carrying a suitcase that matches the leather fragments we were able to find at the point of origin of the explosion. We might get something useful."

Lucky didn't like the possibility that they might not succeed. He had to find that bomber. Better yet, he had to prove the bomber was either Dexter or someone connected to him. And then, he had to stop this SOB before Marin and Noah were put in harm's way again.

From the other side of the glass, Noah grinned at him, a reminder of just what was at stake here.

"I want a copy of those surveillance disks," Lucky requested.

"I figured you would. And I thought about how many different ways to tell you no. You're no longer a cop, Lucky. I can't give you official authorization to see them."

Lucky cursed. "Then I hope you've worked out a way to do it unofficially because I need those disks. Someone tried to kill me, and I want to know who."

Cal groaned heavily enough for Lucky to hear it. "And that's how I'm going to get around the official part. A set of the disks are already on the way to the local sheriff there in Willow Ridge. He'll bring them out to you so you can view them as a witness looking for anything that you would consider suspicious."

Lucky released the breath that he didn't even know he'd been holding. "Thanks, Cal. I owe you."

"Yeah. You do. You can repay me by finding our unknown suspect on those disks." And with that assignment, Cal hung up.

Lucky didn't waste any time. He went back into the sunroom so he could question Helen about Dexter. So far, she was the only person who seemed to want to talk about Marin's brother. But when Lucky saw Marin's face, he immediately knew his questions about Dexter would have to wait.

"What's wrong?" he asked. He hadn't thought it possible, but she was even paler than she had been when they first arrived.

Marin exchanged an uneasy glance with her grandmother, who still had Noah in her arms. "There was a message left for me." She pointed to the phone on a wicker coffee table.

"It's a private line," Helen supplied, taking up the explanation. "Lois didn't have the line taken out when Marin moved. And since no one other than the cleaning lady ever goes out here, we didn't notice the message until just now."

Since this "message" had obviously upset both women, Lucky went to the phone and pressed the play button. It took a couple of seconds to work through Marin's old recorded greeting and the date and time of the call. Two days earlier at nine fifty-three in the morning. About the same time Marin had been on the train en route to Willow Ridge.

The answering machine continued, and a man's rusty voice poured through the sunroom. "Marin Sheppard, this is Grady Duran."

The very person who'd hounded Marin when she first moved to Dallas–Fort Worth.

"I'm tired of waiting for you to get chatty about Dexter," Duran continued. "And I'm tired of warning you of what could happen if you don't tell me where your brother is. My number will be on your caller ID. Get in touch with me. That's not a suggestion. Keep ignoring me, and you'll regret it."

Lucky felt the inevitable slam of anger. How dare this SOB threaten Marin, especially after everything she'd been through. But then, something else occurred to him.

Had Grady Duran been the one to set that explosive? Lucky couldn't immediately see a motive for that, since Duran would want Marin alive. Well, alive until he got the info about Dexter's whereabouts. But maybe the explosion had been meant to scare her.

If so, it'd worked.

"Has Grady Duran ever been here at the ranch?" he asked Helen and Marin.

Marin shook her head. "I don't think so." Helen echoed the same.

Lucky took out his wallet, fished out the dog-eared photo and handed it to Helen. "Does he look familiar?"

Helen brought it closer to her face and studied the picture. Marin leaned in and looked at it, as well. Lucky had already studied it so long that he'd memorized every little detail. Kinley had sent it to him just a month before she was murdered.

The last picture taken of her.

Kinley was smiling, as usual. It was a victory photo of sorts, she'd said in her brief e-mail to Lucky. An office party to celebrate her boss getting a new research contract, which meant she'd be employed at least another year.

In the posed shot, her boss, Dexter, was on her right. Tall, blond and toned, he looked as if he'd be more at home on a California beach than a research lab. He was sporting a thousand-watt smile—smiles like that had probably gone a long way to helping him with the ladies.

Lucky also knew something else about that photo: Dexter had his arm slung a little too intimately over Kinley's shoulder.

On Kinley's left was a woman with light brown hair.

Brenna Martel, Dexter's former lover and other lab assistant. And then there was Grady Duran, standing just off from the others. Wide shoulders, imposing dark stare, he wasn't looking like a man in a festive mood.

Odd, since of the four he was the only one who wasn't missing or dead.

"I remember her," Helen tapped Brenna's image. "Dexter brought her here a time or two. She's dead."

"Looks that way. Either that or she disappeared from the face of the earth. No one's touched her bank accounts or her other personal assets since the night of the explosion at the research facility. What about the other guy, Grady Duran? Ever seen him?"

"He wasn't at the ranch," Helen concluded. "But I'm pretty sure I saw him in town. He was in the parking lot of Doc Sullivan's office when I came out from having my blood pressure checked. That was Monday. I noticed because we don't get many strangers in Willow Ridge, especially this time of year."

Helen turned back to Lucky. "Is it a bad thing that this man's in town?"

"A suspicious thing," Lucky supplied. He didn't like the timing of Duran's reappearance. Monday was the day before the train explosion. "Did he say anything to you?"

"Not a word. In fact, he looked away and turned his head when I spotted him."

Lucky didn't care for that, either. Except that it could mean that Duran was here because he knew Dexter was nearby. That was both good and bad.

He looked at Noah, who had hardly been out of his

arms for two days. Two days wasn't that long. But it was more than long enough. Lucky loved Noah. He couldn't have loved him more if he were his own son. With Dexter's possible return, that meant Lucky would have the additional challenge of protecting Noah in case something went wrong.

"You need to tell the sheriff that you saw this man," Lucky instructed Helen. "And while you're doing that, I'll ask him to keep a watch out for Duran in case he makes a return visit. I don't want him anywhere near here."

Helen's forehead bunched up. "You think there could be trouble?"

"Maybe."

But the truth was trouble was already on the way.

Chapter Seven

Frustrated, Marin shut the dresser drawer with far more force than necessary. "Where is it?" she mumbled.

She'd looked at every inch of the furniture and still hadn't found an eavesdropping device. She glanced at Lucky, who was still examining her closet, but he didn't seem to be having any better luck than she was.

With Noah now asleep in his crib in the sitting room, Marin walked toward the closet. "Maybe Grandma was wrong about the bug," she whispered.

Lucky, too, was obviously frustrated, and he stopped his search to stare at her. "We could be going about this the wrong way," he said under his breath. "Maybe we should just blow off this bug and concentrate on making sure this place is as secure as it can be."

"You've already done that," she pointed out.

The sheriff, Jack Whitley, had already been alerted about Grady Duran possibly being in town, and he'd agreed to send out a deputy to patrol the ranch. The ranch hands had been instructed to keep an eye out for Grady, as well. And her parents had agreed to turn on the security system that they'd had installed but almost never used.

"I could arrange to have surveillance cameras brought in," Lucky explained, his voice not so soft now. "Then, I could monitor the perimeter of the ranch."

"The ranch is huge. Well over a thousand acres and with more than a dozen outbuildings." She glanced back at Noah to make sure he was okay. He was. Her son was on his side and still asleep. "Besides, we only have two days here. After that, I can make other arrangements for security."

Marin was still undecided about her future living arrangements. But returning to Fort Worth probably wasn't a wise move. She'd need a new place, a new home, far away from danger and from her parents. First though, she had to fight this custody challenge.

And she had to keep Noah safe.

Of course, Lucky had taken over that task as if he'd been ordained to protect her son. She couldn't exactly fault him for that. Yes, he'd lied to her about Dexter. Probably lied about hitting on her, as well. But she couldn't doubt that he had her son's best interest at heart.

"So, what do we do about this bug?" Marin mouthed.

Lucky glanced around. Scowled. "Howard and Lois?" he called out. "If you're listening, and you probably are, maybe the judge and the shrink would like to know how perverted you are. Eavesdropping on your daughter having sex with her fiancé. How sick is that, huh?"

Lucky stepped closer to her, placed his palm on the

wall just behind her head, and made a throaty grunting sound. It was the exaggerated sound of a man in the throes of sex. He grunted some more, and Marin couldn't help it, she smiled.

Since she figured this was an impromptu outlet for all that pent-up frustration about her parents' antics, she added some moans of her own.

Lucky laughed. It was husky, low and totally male. And she didn't know why—maybe it was the sheer absurdity of their situation—but their charade did indeed help ease some of the frustration.

Well, for a moment or two.

Then, the frustration returned and went in a totally different direction. Or rather, a too familiar, dangerous direction.

Their eyes met and their gazes held. There it was again, that jolt of attraction that'd hit her when she first met him. Lucky was hot. But Marin remembered he was hands-off. He wanted her brother, and he'd been willing to use her to find him.

That reminder was still flashing through her head when Lucky lowered his head. She saw it coming. He was making a move on her. Slick. Effortless. Still, even though she saw it coming, she didn't do anything to stop it. She leaned closer into him, and his mouth found hers, letting the dreamy feel of his kiss wash over her.

He was gentle. A surprise. She'd thought he would be rough and demanding. A bad boy's kiss. But his mouth was as easy as his smooth Texas drawl.

Marin slipped her arms around his neck. First one, then the other. Everything inside her slowed to practically a crawl. Except her heart. It was racing, and she could feel it in her throat.

The slow crawling feeling didn't last long. It couldn't. Not with his clever kiss. When she'd first seen Lucky's face, she'd thought of him being in a bar brawl, of his rough exterior. Of those snug jeans that hugged all the interesting parts of his body. Now, all of that came into play. All of those had drawn her in.

Her body went from mindless resistance to being flooded with raging heat. His chest brushed her breasts. It was enough to urge her closer, to feel more of him. He was solid, all sinew and muscle, and she felt so soft in his arms.

He hooked his arm around her waist and snapped her to him. The gentleness vanished. Thank goodness! Because what good was it to lust after a rough and tumble bad boy if he held back one of the very things that made him bad?

Their bodies met head-on, a collision of sensations. The thoroughness of his touch. The firmness of his grip. His taste. The undeniable need of his mouth as he took the kiss and made it French.

Yes! she thought. Yes. This was her fantasy. Him, taking her like this. Not treating her with kid gloves.

And Lucky didn't disappoint.

His left hand went into her hair. Avoiding her injured forehead, he caught the strands of hair between his fingers and pulled back her head gently, but firmly so that he controlled the angle of the kiss. So that he controlled her.

Marin moved into the kiss, against him. Lucky

moved, too, sliding his hand down her back, over her butt. He caught on to the back of her thigh, lifting it, just a little, to create the right angle so that his sex would touch hers.

Her breath vanished, and her vision blurred. She mumbled a word of profanity that she'd never used.

Every part of her responded. A slow, melting heat that urged her to take this farther. She wanted Lucky. Not just his French kiss. Not just the clever pressure created by his erection now nestled against her. She wanted it all.

Right here. Right now.

Senseless and thinking with her body, Marin fought to regain control. It wasn't easy. She had to fight her way though the mindlessness of pure, raw desire and a fantasy she'd been weaving for hours. She remembered that having sex just wasn't a good idea. Thankfully, she got a jolt of help when she heard the bedroom door open.

"Noah," she said on a rise of breath.

Just like that, the heat was gone, and even though she turned to race back into the bedroom, Lucky launched himself ahead of her and beat her to it. However, the threat Marin had been prepared to face wasn't there.

Well, not exactly.

With a large thick envelope tucked beneath her arm, her mother, Lois, waltzed inside. Marin made a mental note to keep the door locked from now on—and to keep some distance between Lucky and her.

Lois glanced over at her grandson in the sitting room and gave the sleeping baby a thin smile. Her scrutiny of Lucky and her though lasted a bit longer, and Marin didn't think it was her imagination that her mother was displeased about something. Probably because both Lucky and she looked as if, well, they'd gotten lucky. For the sake of the facade, Marin tried to hang on to the well-satisfied look. It wasn't hard to do. That kiss had been darn memorable.

Which was exactly why she had to forget it.

Her mother snapped her fingers and in stepped a young dark-haired woman carrying a large tray of plates covered with domed silver lids. She set the tray on the desk in the corner and made a hasty exit.

"Your dinner," Lois announced. "Since you made it clear that you wouldn't be dining with us. There's some rice cereal and formula there for Noah, as well."

"Thank you," Lucky responded. "But Noah's already had his dinner—Grandmother brought it in. Oh, and next time, knock first."

Her mother looked as if she wanted to argue with that, but she didn't. Instead, she extracted the envelope and thrust it at Lucky. "Sheriff Whitley had his deputy bring this over for you. I suppose it's connected to the explosion?"

Neither Lucky nor Marin confirmed that. Nor would they. But it was no doubt the surveillance disks from the train that Lucky had told her about. Lucky examined the red tape that sealed the envelope, and Marin could see that someone had written their initials in permanent marker on that tape.

The sound her mother made was of obvious disapproval. "The sheriff apparently packaged it like that. He said if the seal was tampered with that he'd arrest my husband and me for obstruction of justice."

"Good for Sheriff Whitley," Lucky mumbled.

"The man isn't fit to wear that badge," Lois declared. But her expression softened when she looked at Marin. "You should at least eat dinner with your family."

"I would if my family were really a family." Marin paused a moment to put a chokehold on her temper. She didn't want to shout with Noah in the room. "Drop this interview. Apologize. Back off. And then I might have dinner with you."

"The interview has to happen, for your son's sake," her mother said without hesitation. "And it's for his sake that I can't back off."

"Neither can I," someone echoed. It was her father who stepped inside to join forces with her mother.

"Oh, goody," Marin mumbled.

Lucky placed the envelope on the foot of the bed and positioned himself closer to her, so that they were literally facing down her parents.

"By the way, did either of you know about the threatening phone message that Grady Duran left Marin on her private line?" Lucky asked.

It was a good question. One that Marin should have already thought to ask.

"That message," her father grumbled. "Marin's grandmother told us about it after her visit with you. No. We didn't know. But the sheriff does now. For all the good that'll do."

Apparently, her father wasn't any happier with the sealed envelope than her mother. Marin didn't care. She wanted the authorities to know about Grady Duran because it was her guess that he was the one responsible for that explosion, and she wanted him off the streets and behind bars.

Her father propped his hands on his hips. "I thought you should know, I just heard from your brother."

Marin could have sworn her heart stopped.

Lucky must have had a similar reaction because he didn't utter a word. Neither did her mother. And the three all stood there, staring at the man who'd just made the announcement she'd never thought she would hear.

"Dexter's not dead?" Marin finally managed to say.

"Obviously not. He just e-mailed me," Howard explained.

Lois pressed her hand to her chest and pulled in several quick breaths. "What did he say?"

"That he's alive and he wants to come home to see his family."

"Where is he?" Lucky demanded.

"Even if he had said, I wouldn't tell you. Dexter's worried about his safety, as he should be. He knows someone killed two of his employees and an agent who was posing as a security guard at the research facility. Whoever did that is trying to set him up to take the blame."

Marin figured Lucky wasn't buying that or this entire conversation.

Her father's eyes narrowed when he looked at Lucky. "But Dexter says he won't come while you're here, Randall. And he wants you to leave immediately."

It was another shock. Not that Dexter wanted to

come home. But that he'd even mentioned Randall, Marin's dead ex-boyfriend.

"I want to see that e-mail," Lucky insisted.

"I'm sure you do," her father snarled. "But first I want you to answer one question. Since you've supposedly never met anyone in Marin's family, mind explaining how the hell my son knows you?"

Chapter Eight

How the hell does my son know you?

Lucky hadn't been able to provide an answer to Howard Sheppard, nor had he speculated to the man. He'd ended the inquisition by walking away. Now, two hours later, he still didn't know the answer to Howard's question.

Was the e-mail bogus? And if it was real, did that mean Dexter knew who Lucky really was and why he was at the ranch?

Of course, another possibility was that Howard had asked Dexter to make that demand. After all, what better and faster way to get Lucky off the ranch than to tie Dexter's homecoming to his departure? It would give Howard and Lois everything they wanted.

Their son's return.

And their daughter and grandson at the ranch with no ally, other than Marin's grandmother, who was too old to put up much of a fight. After all, Helen hadn't been able to stop the Sheppards so far. That's why Lucky had refused to leave and then ordered Marin's parents out of the room.

Well, it was one of the reasons anyway.

That kissing session with Marin was another.

Pushing that uncomfortable thought aside, Lucky concentrated on the images from the surveillance disks on his laptop. So far, he hadn't seen anything or anyone suspicious, and he'd been looking for well over an hour. He'd hoped to have spotted Dexter doing something incriminating by now.

He heard Noah stir, and Lucky got up from the desk to check on him. But Noah was still sleeping peacefully in the crib in the sitting room.

Lucky leaned down, gave Noah a light kiss on the cheek and turned to go back to the bedroom, but another sound stopped him. Marin came out of the bathroom. Toweling her damp hair, she was dressed in a turquoise-blue robe that was nearly the same color as her eyes.

She didn't look so pale now, probably because the hot steamy shower had given her skin a pinkish flush. She'd changed the bandage on her forehead, replacing it was a Band-Aid that covered the stitches. It was less noticeable, even though it still exposed the bruise left from the impact.

"Everything okay?" she asked in a whisper.

He nodded. "Just making sure he's all right."

Marin walked closer, close enough for him to catch her scent. Lucky hadn't remembered strawberry shampoo ever smelling that good.

"It's probably best that you try to distance yourself from him," she said, her voice still soft. "Since you'll only be around him a couple more days, I don't want him to get too attached."

Lucky thought it might be too late for that. For both of them. But Marin was right. Noah wasn't his to claim, even though his feelings for Noah were the most real thing he'd felt since his sister's death. Noah was young and wouldn't remember him, but Lucky would certainly remember the little boy.

"The same applies to us," Marin added, scratching her eyebrow. She shifted her position and adjusted the sash on her robe. "That kiss in the closet shouldn't have happened."

He had to agree with that, even though saying it to himself didn't make the sensations go away.

"I want to kiss you again," he admitted.

Her shoulders snapped back. "But you won't," she insisted, sounding about as convinced as Lucky felt. "We need to keep our hands off each other."

"It's not my hands you should be worried about," he mumbled, causing her to laugh.

"Tell you what, if the kissing urge hits us again," she said, "let's make ourselves count to ten. That might give us just enough time to realize what a huge mistake we'd be making."

Right.

The side of her bathrobe slipped a little, easing off her shoulder. Her *bare* shoulder. And he got just a glimpse of the top of her right breast and her nipple.

"Oh, man. You're not wearing anything beneath that bathrobe?"

She jerked the sides together to close the gap. "I came out to check on Noah. Then, I was going to get dressed."

"So you're naked?"

Why couldn't he just let this subject drop? Because he was suddenly aroused beyond belief.

So, he did something totally stupid. He reached out, caught on to her shoulders.

And yeah, he kissed her again, all the while convincing himself that if he stopped, she'd give into the emotion caused by the danger and the adrenaline. She'd get worried and depressed again. He also tried to convince himself that he wasn't enjoying it, that it was therapeutic.

A bald-faced lie.

He was enjoying the heck out of it. The feel of her mouth against his. The way she fit in his arms. The hot-as-sin scent of hers stirring around him. Yes, he was enjoying it.

And he wasn't the only one.

Marin moaned in pure pleasure. That's when he knew he had to stop. With Noah only a couple of inches away, this couldn't continue.

He pulled away from her, ran his tongue over his bottom lip and wasn't surprised when he tasted her there. It was a taste that might be permanently etched into his brain.

"We shouldn't have done that, either," she grumbled. "With all the emotional baggage that each of us has, it wouldn't work between us. Every time you look at me, you'll see my brother, the man you blame for your sister's death."

"You're right," he said. Except it was partly a lie. Marin would always be Dexter's sister, but she was also her own woman.

And he was attracted to her.

Still, Marin was correct. They shouldn't be kissing. Maybe if he said it enough to himself, his body would start to listen. Heaven knows it hadn't listened to anything else he'd demanded it not do.

Lucky tried to get his mind back on business. "While you were in the shower, I got another call from my friend Cal Rico. He's a special agent in the Justice Department, and he's the one responsible for getting those surveillance disks to the sheriff who got them to me."

"Have you found anything?" she asked.

"Not yet. I'm still looking. But Cal let me know that he's using department resources to look into the e-mail Dexter sent your father."

"I think that e-mail was a hoax. It might be my father's way of trying to get you to leave."

Marin and he were obviously on the same page. "Either way, Cal will find out the origin of the e-mail."

Lucky didn't doubt his friend's ability, but verifying the e-mail was a long shot. If Dexter had indeed sent the e-mail, then he would have almost certainly covered his tracks.

Marin turned and tipped her head toward his laptop. "So, what have you seen on those surveillance disks?"

"A lot of people. Not Dexter though. But if he came onto the train, he was probably wearing a disguise." He paused. "Maybe you could take a look at them and see if you can spot him."

She frowned, then nodded. "All right. But for the record, I don't expect to see him. I think we should be looking for Grady Duran."

"Absolutely. But since you know what he looks like, as well, this might go faster with both of us going over the surveillance." But he rethought that when he glanced at the bandage on her head. "Then again, why don't you get some rest, and I'll finish reviewing the disks."

"I'll help," she insisted, going straight for the desk.

Lucky huffed, but he knew it wouldn't do any good to try to talk her out of this. He was quickly learning that Marin was as stubborn as he was.

That only made him want her more.

"By the way," he whispered, just in case there was a bug in the room. "Are there any extra linens around?" He glanced at the bed as they walked past it. "I'm thinking it's not a good idea if we share the same mattress."

She understood completely. "The extra bedding's in the linen closet. Next to my parents' room. Probably not a good idea to advertise the fact we need two sleeping areas."

True. They already had enough issues with Howard and Lois. "No problem. I'll just take the floor."

"We could build a barrier with the pillows—"

He stopped and stared at her mouth. "I get your point," she conceded. "Pillows wouldn't be much of a barrier."

Heck, he wasn't sure being on the floor would be much of a barrier, either, but Lucky knew he wouldn't get a minute of sleep next to her. And he needed a clear head along with a little sleep to get through the next two days.

Lucky clicked the resume feature on the surveillance

disk, and images immediately appeared on the screen. Marin dragged a chair next to his, and they sat, silently. Since Lucky figured a visual aid might help Marin, he took out the photo of Dexter, Grady Duran, his sister and Brenna Martel and positioned it next to his laptop.

"This is the station in Fort Worth, where we both got on," he explained. "The security cameras were on the entire time that passengers were boarding." He back-tracked the disk to show her the recorded image of Noah and her.

Lucky was about ten yards behind them.

Several times during that brief walk from the terminal to the train, Marin glanced back, but each time Lucky tried to make sure he disappeared in the crowd.

"Well, if I didn't notice you," she remarked, "then I could have missed Grady Duran."

"Or your brother."

That earned him a scowl that he probably deserved, and they continued to watch the disk. "Okay, this is where I left off before I went to check on Noah. The train is about to leave. There are only a couple of people left at the terminal door. And none of them look anything like Grady Duran or Dexter."

"None of those people are carrying a large suitcase, either."

Without taking her attention from the screen, Marin got up, opened a bottle of pills that she'd placed on the dresser and took one of the tablets, washing it down with a glass of water she took from their dinner tray.

"Pain meds?" Lucky questioned.

"No. I took one of those earlier. This is for my

seizures. I have to take them twice a day—a small price to pay for being as normal as I can be."

Yes. It was. But he wondered how all of this additional stress was affecting her health. "How old were you when you had your first seizure?"

"Twelve. I was riding a roller coaster at an amusement park. Scared the devil out of everyone, including myself. Before that, my parents were only over-protective. After that, they got obsessive."

He shrugged. "But you said you haven't had a seizure in years. That should cause them to back off."

"You'd think." She gave a heavy sigh and sank down next to him again. "They do love me in their own crazy way. I know that. But they just can't seem to give up control. They're scared I'll have another seizure, and they won't be around to help me."

Lucky understood that. He'd felt that way about his sister. And now Noah.

Hell, Marin was on that list, too.

Since it was starting to feel like one of those moments where he wanted to pull Marin in his arms and protect the hell out of her, Lucky just turned his focus back the surveillance images.

And then he saw it.

Just as the train was about to close the boarding doors, a passenger carrying a black suitcase hurried forward. Dressed in a bulky knee-length denim coat, the person wore jeans, gloves and a Texas Rangers baseball cap. With that cap sitting low on the forehead and with the bulky clothes, it was hard to tell who the person was.

Lucky backtracked the disk to the point just prior to boarding, froze the frame and zoomed in.

"Does that look like Dexter?" Lucky asked.

Marin moved even closer to the screen and studied it. "No. The body language is wrong. Dexter didn't slump like that."

"Maybe he would if he was trying to keep his face from being seen." Lucky advanced the disk one frame farther and got a better view of the face. Well, the lower part of it anyway. That cap created a strategic shadow.

Marin shook her head. "It's not Dexter. Maybe Grady Duran?"

That was the next possibility that Lucky had planned to consider. He rewound even more of the disk, looking for the best face shot possible. When he thought he'd found it, he zoomed in again. And this time, he didn't have to ask if that was Dexter or Grady Duran.

Because it wasn't either of the men. It wasn't a man at all.

He was looking at the face of a dead woman.

His sister, Kinley.

Chapter Nine

From her chair in the sitting room, Marin finished her scrambled eggs and watched her grandmother feed Noah. Noah and her gran were doing great, but she couldn't say the same for Lucky.

He still hadn't moved.

He'd been at that desk in the adjoining bedroom for at least two hours, and it didn't appear he was going to move anytime soon. Right now, he was on hold, waiting for Agent Cal Rico to come back on the line. With his cell phone sandwiched between his shoulder and ear, his fingers worked frantically on the keyboard of his laptop. What he wasn't doing was eating his breakfast.

Marin stood, put her mug of tea aside and blew Noah and her grandmother a kiss. She went into the bedroom toward the desk. "Why don't you come with me for a walk?" she suggested to Lucky.

He didn't even glance up at her. He kept his attention superglued to the e-mail he was typing on the computer screen. "You should be resting."

"It's 9:00 a.m. I've already rested. You, on the other

hand, haven't. I know for a fact that you didn't get much sleep. You were in the bathroom talking on your cell phone most of the night."

"I'm sorry I kept you up," he grumbled.

She huffed. "I'm concerned about you, not me."

He huffed, too. "I'm not tired."

Oh, yes, he was. And he was frustrated and confused. Marin totally understood why. Before last night, all the evidence pointed to his dead sister having had no part in the wrongdoing at the research facility. But yet there she was in that surveillance video.

"I'm still here," Lucky quickly said into the phone. Agent Cal Rico had obviously come back on the line, hopefully with some answers.

Lucky paused. "I need your lab to keep trying to enhance that image from the disk." Another pause. "Yeah, I'm asking the impossible, but I have to know if that was Kinley getting onto the train."

Another pause, but she could see that Lucky was processing something. "Bits of money?" he questioned. "And you're sure that was in the suitcase, along with some clothes. Just how big was that explosive device anyway?"

Marin couldn't hear the agent's answer, but after several terse answers from Lucky, he jabbed the end-call button and cursed. He lowered his voice to mumble profanity, however, when his attention landed on Helen feeding Noah rice cereal for breakfast. Marin figured there was more cereal on her son and her grandmother than in Noah's tummy.

Noah grinned when he realized he had everyone's

attention, and Lucky gave him a half-hearted smile in return before he groaned and rubbed his eyes.

That did it. Marin caught on to his arm, and in the same motion, she took his leather jacket from the back of the chair. "We're taking that walk," she insisted.

Lucky stood but didn't move. His stare was a challenge, and it let her know that he had no plans to budge.

"There are things we need to discuss," she whispered. "And I'd prefer not to do that in a room that's bugged. Plus, I could use some fresh air."

He glanced at his laptop, his silent cell phone and then at Noah.

"A *short* walk," Lucky finally conceded. "I don't want you out in that cold very long."

Marin didn't argue with the restriction. She turned toward the sitting room, but before she could even ask her grandmother if she'd watch Noah for a couple of minutes, the woman was already nodding. "Go ahead. Take as much time as you need."

She thanked her grandmother, grabbed her coat from the closet, put it on and led Lucky out the enclosed patio exit before he could change his mind.

Thankfully, it wasn't nearly as cold as it had been the day before. Still, it was in the low fifties, and Marin hugged her coat close to her so that she wouldn't get a chill.

"About an hour ago, I called a lawyer that I know in Fort Worth," Marin explained. "I asked him to contact the psychologist to see if he'd cancel the interview since I don't feel it's necessary."

"Don't count on that happening. The psychologist is probably in your parents' pockets, as well."

That might be true, but Marin had to try. Lucky wasn't in the right state of mind for that interview. Neither was she, and Marin hoped there was still some way to prevent it from happening.

She spotted her mother staring at them from the window, and Marin maneuvered him away from the yard and onto a trail that would take them to the edge of the one of the pastures. "Either way, I want you to leave this morning so you can find your sister."

He tossed her a puzzling glance. "Leave? If I don't do that interview, Marin, you could lose Noah."

Yes, and that terrified her. Still, she couldn't make Lucky stay, not when he had so much at stake. "But if you don't look for your sister before the trail goes cold, you might not find her."

"If that's really my sister."

So, he had doubts, as well. "You're thinking it's a look-alike?"

He shrugged. "I'm thinking if my sister had been alive for the past year, then she would have already contacted me."

"I seem to remember saying the same thing to you about Dexter."

"But my sister wasn't doing anything illegal." Then, he frowned. "At least, I don't think she was."

Neither was Marin. Anything was possible. "Let's assume then that it was a look-alike, maybe even someone in disguise. Brenna Martel, maybe?"

"No. I'd recognize Brenna." He said it so quickly that he'd obviously already considered it. "Plus, there's also the issue of the blood. Both Brenna's and my sister's blood was found all over the floor in Dexter's research lab. The CSI guys said there was little chance that the women could have survived after losing that much blood."

But survival was possible. And that led Marin to the next question. "Was the suitcase the woman was carrying the one that contained the explosives?"

"It appears to be. It also contained money and clothes. Agent Rico believes the explosives were hidden in a concealed compartment."

Since they'd already ruled out the logical explanations, Marin tried out one that was unlikely but still possible. "So, maybe your sister is alive. Maybe she has amnesia from her injuries at the research facility? That would explain why she hasn't contacted you."

"But it wouldn't explain why she got on that train."

Good point. Marin quickly tried to come up with something to counter that. "Maybe she didn't know she was carrying explosives?"

"I considered that at about 1:00 a.m. when I checked the records of everyone injured. There was no injured woman fitting my sister's description. If she hadn't known she was carrying explosives, then she would have been sitting near the suitcase."

"Perhaps not. She could have gone to the bathroom or something. She could have changed seats for a variety of reasons. Like maybe some guy was hitting on her."

The corner of his mouth lifted for a very short smile.

He stopped at a small rocky stream that cut through the pasture. The water created a miniature valley and was banked with chunks of white limestone and slate-gray clay. It was a peaceful spot where she'd spent a lot of time as a kid. A bare pasture was on one side and in the spring would be filled with Angus cattle that would graze there. On the other side was a barn that stored equipment, tractors and massive circular bales of hay.

Lucky could have easily stepped over the stream, but instead he stared into the water. "I want to believe she's alive and that she's done nothing wrong. That'd be the best-case scenario. But even if Kinley has amnesia or whatever, she obviously needs help."

If Grady Duran was gutsy enough to press Marin for answers about Dexter, how hard would he press Kinley? Lucky's sister could be in danger.

"Let's go back to the house," Marin insisted. "I'll have someone drive you to the train station, the airport or wherever you need to go to find her."

He continued to look into the water. "That would make your parents very happy. They'd have you right where they want you. Here, alone and in fear of losing your son."

"I won't lose Noah," she promised. "I'll figure out a way to postpone or cancel that meeting." Though Marin didn't have a clue how she was going to do that. "Besides, the lawyer in Fort Worth is sending someone down to talk to the judge and the psychologist."

"If all that fails, you'd be giving up a lot," he said. "Just so I can leave."

He was thinking of her. Well, maybe more Noah than her. But whichever, he was putting himself and his needs after hers.

And Marin couldn't help but appreciate that.

There it was. That weird intimacy again. It was growing. They seemed to be racing toward some heated passionate encounter that neither of them seemed capable of stopping.

Worse, she wasn't sure she wanted to stop it.

He reached out and brushed his hand over her arm. Even through the wool coat, she could feel his touch. Then, he trailed those clever fingers over her cheek. The moment was far warmer than it should have been.

But then, Lucky's hand froze.

"What's wrong?" Marin asked.

He didn't answer. He didn't have to. Marin heard the thick roar of the engine and looked in the direction of the sound. A large rust-scabbed tan-colored truck with heavily tinted windows bolted out from the barn.

Her first thought was a ranch hand had loaded the truck bed with hay to take out to one of the other pastures. But there was no hay. The driver, hidden behind all that dark glass, gunned the engine.

The truck came right at them.

LUCKY'S HEART DROPPED. This couldn't be happening.

He drew his weapon and hooked his arm around Marin's waist. He didn't wait to see if that truck was the threat that he thought it was.

Waiting was too big of a risk.

Firing shots through that windshield might not be the best idea, either, because shooting would mean stopping to take aim. The driver could be low in the seat, or leaning far to the side, out of range. Lucky couldn't stand there and shoot when he might not even hit the guy. He had to get Marin out of the path of the oncoming vehicle and then figure out if he needed to stop the driver.

They jumped the shallow stream, and ran like hell. He hoped the soggy clay banks would be enough to slow down the truck.

It wasn't.

The four-wheel drive went right through it, sloshing rocks and water out from the mammoth-size tires.

So Lucky did the only thing he could do. He continued to run and pulled Marin right along with him.

Glancing back over his shoulder, Lucky tried to assess their situation. It damn sure wasn't good. That truck was closing in fast. And there was literally no place to hide in an open pasture. Their best bet was to try to double back and get to the barn.

Easier said that done.

The truck was in their path and coming straight for them. And it was quickly eating up the meager distance between them.

"Go right," Lucky yelled to Marin, hoping that she heard him over the roar of the engine.

Just in case she didn't, Lucky dragged her in the direction he wanted her to go.

The driver adjusted, and came at them again.

"Who's doing this?" Marin shouted.

But Lucky didn't have to time to speculate. Marin and he had to sprint to their right. The truck was so close that Lucky could feel the heat from the engine. And the front bumper missed them by less than a couple of inches.

Marin stumbled. Lucky's heart did, too. But he didn't let her fall. A fall could be fatal for both of them. Instead, he grabbed her and zigzagged to their left.

It wasn't enough.

The driver came right at them, and to avoid being hit, Lucky latched on to Marin even tighter and dove out of the way.

They landed hard on the packed winter soil.

Lucky came up, ready to fire. "Run!" he shouted to Marin.

Thankfully, she managed to do that and started sprinting toward the barn. The truck had to turn around and backtrack to come at him again. Those few precious seconds of time might be the only break they got.

So, Lucky took aim at the windshield and fired.

A thick blast tore through the pasture, drowning out even the sound of the roaring truck engine. The bullet slammed into the safety glass and shattered it, but it stayed in place, concealing the identity of the driver.

Maybe someone from the house would hear the shot and come running. But the house was a good quarter of a mile away, and it might take Marin's parents or the ranch hands a couple of minutes just to figure out what was going on.

By then, they could be dead.

Lucky dodged another attempt to run him down, repositioned himself and fired again. This bullet skipped off the truck's roof and sent sparks flying when it ripped through the metal. What it didn't do was stop the driver.

The truck came at him again.

Lucky dove out of the way. But not before the front bumper scraped against his right thigh.

He fired another shot into the windshield and prayed he could stop the SOB who was trying to kill them.

From the corner of his eye, Lucky spotted Marin running toward the barn. She looked over her shoulder at him, and he could see the terror on her face. Still, she was alive, and the driver didn't appear to be going after her.

Lucky dove for the ground again, but just like before, the driver adjusted and swung back around. He figured if he could keep this up until Marin got to the barn, then maybe she could call for help.

But on the next turn, the driver changed course. He didn't come after Lucky. He did a doughnut in the pasture and slammed on the accelerator.

Hell. He was going after Marin.

She was still a good thirty feet from the barn, and even once inside, she might not be protected. This SOB might just drive the truck right in there after her. If that happened, she'd be trapped.

There was no way he could outrun the truck and get to Marin first, so Lucky took aim again and fired. This time, the back windshield blew apart, and he got just a glimpse of the driver.

Whoever it was wore a dark knit cap.

Lucky fired again. And again. Until he saw the truck's brake lights flash on. Maybe one of the shots had hit him. Lucky hoped so. But just in case this was some kind of ploy to make them think he was hurt, Lucky kept his gun aimed, and he raced forward.

Ahead of him, with the truck at a dead stop in between them, Marin ducked into the barn. Thank God. She might be safer there.

Lucky raced forward, keeping his eye on the driver and looking out for any weapon the guy might have.

Lucky slowed when he neared the truck and kept his gun ready. "Step out of the vehicle," Lucky warned.

He needed the guy out in the open because he could be just sitting there waiting for his best opportunity to kill Lucky so he could go after Marin.

Nothing.

No reaction. No sound.

Not even any movement.

Lucky inched forward. And with each step he prayed he wouldn't look inside that vehicle and see his sister. If she'd been the one on that train, if she'd set those explosives, then she might want him dead. Why, he didn't know. And he didn't want to have to find out.

He took another step, then another—aware that between the pulse hammering in his ears and the drone of the engine, he couldn't hear much. But he didn't need to hear well to realize that the driver was about to do something that Lucky was certain he wouldn't like.

The brake lights went off. In the same second, the driver jammed the accelerator again.

"No!" Lucky yelled.

He added another prayer that Marin had found some safe place in the barn.

To his right, he heard voices. Someone shouting their names. Two of the ranch hands were making their way across the pasture. Neither was armed, but because they were closer to the barn, Lucky figured they would stand a better chance of getting to Marin in time.

The driver must have thought so, as well. Because he didn't head for the barn.

Instead, he made a beeline for the back of the pasture, obviously trying get away.

"Take care of Marin," Lucky shouted to the ranch hands as he started sprinting after the truck.

Chapter Ten

Marin glanced at the clock on the nightstand next to her bed. It was less than a minute since the last time she'd checked. It felt like an eternity, but it had only been a little over an hour that Sheriff Whitley and Lucky had been searching for the driver of that truck.

Maybe Lucky and the sheriff had already caught the man. Maybe he was already on his way to the jail, ready to tell the sheriff why he wanted her dead.

"Maybe," she mumbled.

She hugged Noah to her chest and rocked him. After nearly being killed in the pasture, she needed to hold her son and try to deal with the adrenaline shock and the aftermath.

"He's asleep," her grandmother whispered. "Want me to put him in his crib?"

Marin was about to decline, to say she wanted another minute or two to hold Noah, but then she heard footsteps. Because the overwhelming sense of danger was still with her, she bolted from the bed, ready to run so that she could protect her baby. But running wasn't necessary.

Lucky appeared in the doorway.

"The driver got away," he announced.

So much for her wish. "But the truck left tracks. The sheriff will be able to follow him."

Lucky shook his head. "The truck drove through a fence in the back of the pasture, and Sheriff Whitley thinks he escaped using an old ranch trail."

So, he was gone. Gone! And that meant Lucky, Noah and she weren't safe. There could be another attack.

Her grandmother came and took Noah, gently removing him from her arms, and carried him into the sitting room. Since Marin didn't want to wake him and they obviously had to talk, she grabbed on to his arm and led him into her walk-in closet.

"I'm sorry," Lucky mumbled. "I should have caught that SOB while he was still in the pasture."

His frustration and anger were so strong they were palatable. Marin knew how he felt. "He was in a truck. You were on foot. Catching him was a long shot at best."

She hoped her words comforted her as much as she was trying to comfort Lucky. This wasn't his fault. In fact, he'd done everything in his power to stop her from being hurt. He had literally put himself in harm's way to protect her.

"Are you okay?" he asked. He leaned away from her and checked her over from head to toe.

"I'm fine." Marin checked him, as well, and wasn't pleased to see grass and mud on his jacket and jeans. But then, he'd had to hit the ground several times to dodge the truck. "Were you hurt?"

"No." There was a thin veneer of bravado covering all the emotion that lay just beneath the surface. Lucky held on to his composure for several seconds before he cursed. "First the explosion. Now, this. I brought all of this to your doorstep."

"I doubt it." She touched his arm and rubbed gently. "Since this particular doorstep at the ranch is also Dexter's, the danger might have happened whether you were here or not."

She saw the flash of realization in his eyes, and he glanced over his shoulder in the direction of the sitting room, where her son was sleeping. When Lucky's gaze came back to hers, there was a different emotion. One she understood because she was a parent.

Lucky cursed again and pulled her to him. His grip was too tight. His breath, hot and fast. She felt his heartbeat hammer against her chest.

He mumbled something she didn't understand. The words came out as mere breath brushing against her hair.

"I didn't get a good a look at the driver of that truck," he said. "Did you?"

"No. But I don't think it was Dexter." Marin immediately reexamined the images racing through her head. "Still, I can't be sure, especially since I didn't see the driver's face." She paused. "First there was that e-mail from Dexter. And then you see Kinley on the surveillance video. Two of the people we thought were dead might not be."

He nodded. "Now the question is, are they responsible for what's happening to us?" Lucky also paused. "But just like you can't believe Dexter would do this, I can't believe Kinley would, either."

Neither of them could be objective about the situation. Marin knew that. But it didn't mean they were wrong. Maybe both of their siblings were alive.

And innocent.

There was a sharp knock at the bedroom door, and Lucky drew his gun from his shoulder holster. He headed out of the closet. Fast. He obviously wasn't taking any chances. But the vigilance was unnecessary because the person on the other side of the door was Sheriff Jack Whitley.

Marin had known Jack most of her life, and he hadn't changed much. A real cowboy cop. Tall and lanky with dark hair and gray eyes, Jack had on jeans and a white shirt with his badge clipped onto a leather belt.

Since Jack obviously wanted to talk to them, Marin thought of the bug, and her parents who were probably trying to hear every word. "We'll have some privacy out here," she told him, and Jack didn't say anything until they walked into the enclosed patio.

"My deputy wasn't able to find the truck or the driver," Jack announced, causing Lucky to groan. The sheriff volleyed glances at them and kept his voice low. "You're sure this guy tried to kill you?"

"Dead sure," Lucky insisted.

Jack nodded and seemed to accept that as gospel truth. "The ranch hands said the truck wasn't used very often and was put in the barn for the winter. Keys were almost certainly in the ignition, and the barn wasn't locked, either. They didn't see anyone around that part of the pasture."

"I guess that means no one saw the driver?" she asked.

"No one," Jack Whitley verified. "But there were footprints in the barn, and there's a Texas Ranger coming out from the crime lab. He'll take impressions and try to see if that'll tell us anything." His attention landed on Marin. "I spoke to your dad. He says this has nothing to do with Dexter."

It took Marin several long moments to figure out how to answer that. "I want to believe that."

Jack didn't answer right away, either. "Yeah. I understand. But since I have a job to do and since I'm sure you don't want to dodge any more trucks, I have to say that the circumstantial evidence is pointing to Dexter."

"Why do you say that?" Lucky wanted to know.

The sheriff took out the envelope he had tucked beneath his arm. "A visitor who just arrived and this." He extracted a photo from the envelope and handed it to Lucky.

Marin leaned in so she could see the photograph, as well. It was a grainy shot, taken from what appeared to be the surveillance camera outside the bank on Main Street. But even with the grainy shot, it wasn't hard to make out the woman's face.

"That's Brenna Martel," Lucky confirmed. "She's someone else I thought was dead."

Jack made a sound of agreement. "While I was looking around for that truck driver, I had the Justice Department give me a case update." Now, his attention turned to Lucky. "I know who you really are. And it seems your sister and now this woman might both be alive. Dexter, too."

Three people, all presumed dead. Now, all alive. Innocent people didn't usually let their friends and families believe they were dead unless something bad, very bad, was going on.

"You said something about a visitor?" Lucky prompted.

Marin held her breath. God, had one of those three come to the ranch?

"The visitor is the other player in the case," Jack explained. "Grady Duran."

"He's here?" And Lucky didn't sound any happier about it than Marin was.

"Duran's here," the sheriff verified. "And he's demanding to speak to both of you now."

LUCKY WOULD HAVE preferred to delay this meeting.

After all, Marin was just coming down from a horrible ordeal. The last thing he wanted was to add any more tension to her already stress-filled day. But this chat with Duran might give them answers, and right now, answers were in very short supply.

"I'd rather you waited in the bedroom," Lucky repeated to Marin. But like the other two times he'd said it, she didn't budge. She walked side by side with him toward the front of the ranch house where the sheriff had said Grady Duran was waiting to see them. Sheriff Whitley was right behind them.

"If Duran's the one who just tried to kill us, then I want the chance to confront him," Marin insisted.

That's what Lucky was afraid of. That Duran had indeed been behind the wheel of the truck. And that Duran would try to kill them again.

But why?

Lucky kept going back to that critical question. If Duran was on the up and up and simply wanted answers as to Dexter's whereabouts, then he wouldn't want Marin and him dead. He'd follow them, demand to talk to them. But it would serve no purpose for Duran to kill them.

Well, at least no purpose that Lucky could think of.

Still, he couldn't take any more risks when it came to Marin. As they approached the great room of the ranch house, Lucky drew his weapon. He checked over his shoulder and saw that the sheriff had placed his hand over the butt on his own service revolver. Good. They were both ready in case something went wrong.

Duran was pacing in the great room. The man was just over six feet tall and solid. He wore a perfectly tailored suit. Cashmere, probably. He impatiently checked his watch at the exact moment his gaze connected with Lucky's.

Duran wasn't alone. On the other side of the massive room near the stone fireplace stood Lois and Howard Sheppard. They didn't look happy about their unexpected visitor.

"He said it was important, that it's about Dexter," Lois volunteered. "I was hoping he'd know where my son is. That's the only reason we let him in." She didn't go any closer to her daughter. Probably because both the sheriff and Lucky moved protectively in front of Marin.

However, Marin would have no part in that. She merely stepped to the side. "Were you the one who tried to kill us?" she demanded.

"No," Duran readily answered, though the denial hadn't come easily. The muscles in his jaw were so tight that Lucky was surprised the man could even speak. "I could ask you the same thing. Someone planted an explosive device in my rental car."

Lucky glanced at the sheriff who confirmed that with a nod. "The device was on a timer, but failed to detonate. If it had, I would have been blown to smithereens."

"Well, neither Lucky nor I set an explosive," Marin grumbled. "But I'm sure you're not short of suspects. With your caustic personality, you've made your share of enemies."

Duran didn't react to her insult. He whipped his gaze toward Lois and Howard. "What about you two? Either of you into blowing things up to protect your son?"

Lois made a slight gasp and flattened her hand over her chest. Howard hardly reacted, other than a slight narrowing of his eyes. "I think you've already worn out your welcome."

Duran shook his head. "I'm not leaving yet. Not until you tell me where Dexter is."

"We thought you knew," Lois accused.

Lucky waited for someone to respond, but the room fell silent.

"All right. I'll get this conversation rolling," Duran continued a moment later, aiming his comment at Howard and Lois. "Here's my theory. You want me out of the picture because when I find Dexter, I'm going to haul his butt off to jail. Then, I'll figure out how to get back every penny he owes me. And by the way, that's a lot of pennies. Your son is in debt to me for the tune of nearly six million dollars."

Six million. Lucky had no idea it was that much. That was a big motive for murder. It also explained why Duran was desperate to find Dexter.

Howard took a menacing step forward, but Duran held out his hands. Then, he pulled an envelope from his pocket and slapped it onto the coffee table. "That's a copy of the letter my lawyer sent to the state attorney general and the Justice Department. I haven't had the best relationship with those two groups in the past, but I've decided to help them with their ongoing investigation."

"So?" Howard challenged.

But Lucky knew what this meant, and it had just upped the stakes.

So far, Duran had tried to find Dexter on his own. He'd not only refused to assist the Justice Department, he had likely withheld critical evidence. Now, Duran's cooperation could blow this case wide open, and it could lead them directly to Dexter or at least to the truth of what'd really happened in that research facility.

"*So,*" Duran repeated, "I'd rather deal with Dexter on my own, but I'm willing to cut a deal with the Feds. I'm also willing to hang your son to get revenge for what he did to me. Understand?"

"We understand," Lois snapped.

The corner of Duran's mouth lifted. "I'm not going away. And I'm not backing down. I'm staying in Willow Ridge, and I plan to haunt you, your daughter and her fiancé until you lead me to Dexter."

"Just make sure your threats stay verbal," the sheriff warned Duran. "Because you'll be the one arrested if you cross the line."

Duran mumbled something and turned to leave. Lucky followed him. Marin would have no doubt done the same, but the phone rang, and several seconds later, one of the housekeepers announced that the call was for Marin.

Lucky went to the porch and caught Duran's arm before he could head down the steps. "Talk to me about Kinley Ford. What do you know about her?"

"She's dead." He paused, studied Lucky's expression and then shook off his grip with far more force than necessary. "At least the police think she is. You have any information to the contrary?"

"No," Lucky lied.

Duran kept staring. "Kinley Ford was at the research facility the night of the explosion. I know, because I was there, too."

"You saw her?" But Lucky already knew the answer. Or rather the answer that Duran had given the investigators when they had first interviewed him.

"I did see her. Dexter, Brenna and Kinley." Duran glanced around the grounds. The vigilant glance of a man who was wary of his surroundings. "Something was off, but I didn't know what. Dexter was acting even less normal than usual. I mean, he was forever pulling that prima donna genius crap where he'd say he couldn't be interrupted. But that night, he was wound up so tight that I could see he was about to snap."

Probably because Dexter was about to put his plan into action. "Did you ask why he was on edge?"

He lifted a shoulder, glanced around again "The prototype of the chemical project was due within forty-eight hours. Dexter kept saying it was ready, but that I couldn't see it until he'd given it one final test." Duran cursed. "I should have forced him to show it to me."

Lucky gave that some thought. "So, if the prototype wasn't ready, you think Dexter could have set the explosion, run with his research project and then faked his death?"

Duran met him eye to eye. "I think he faked not only his own death but maybe Kinley Ford's and Brenna Martel's."

Yes. After seeing his sister on that surveillance video, Lucky had toyed with that idea, too. Still, there was all that blood. "Why would Dexter have done that?"

"Simple. Because he needed their help to finish the project. Plus, he knew what a fortune that chemical weapon would make, and he didn't want to hand it over to the investors. Maybe he thought he could get away with it if everyone associated with the project was presumed dead. Then, he could wait a year or two and use an alias when he tried to sell it on the black market."

"There's a big problem with that theory. Kinley Ford wouldn't have cooperated with Dexter's illegal plan. She wasn't a criminal," Lucky insisted.

Duran shrugged. "Maybe she wasn't a willing participant."

Hell. That theory raced through and left him with more questions than when he'd started this investigation. "What could Dexter have used to force her to cooperate?"

"Right off the top of my head, I'd say maybe she was a fool for love. Brenna certainly was." Another glance around. "But I know that Dexter had already broken things off with Brenna."

Lucky hated to even put this out there, but it was something he had to know. "And you think that Dexter then started an affair with Kinley?"

Another shrug. "Something was going on between them. Hell for all I know, maybe Kinley Ford was the mastermind of that explosion. Or Brenna. *Women,*" he added like profanity.

Lucky dismissed his sister's involvement. He had to. Because he couldn't deal with the alternative. "But if Dexter and both women are alive, why haven't they surfaced?"

"Maybe they have." Duran extracted a set of car keys from his pocket. "My advice? Don't trust anyone around here."

"You think Dexter wants me dead, too?"

Duran blinked. "He has no reason to kill you. Does he?"

Oh, Lucky could think of a reason. If Dexter knew who he really was, then he might try to eliminate him. Dexter would figure out that Lucky wouldn't stop until he had justice for Kinley.

If Kinley needed justice, that is.

Lucky hated that he was beginning to doubt her.

"But I think Dexter's parents would do anything to keep you out of their daughter's life," Duran continued. "The stories Dexter used to tell me about them. They're manipulative enough to be very dangerous." He headed down the steps.

Like Duran, Lucky wasn't certain that Howard and Lois's parental concerns were all just threats.

He turned to go back inside, but as he reached for the door, it opened. Marin was there, and he instantly knew something was wrong. She'd probably gotten some bad news from that phone call.

"Is it your brother?" he asked.

She shook her head. "The psychologist, Dr. Ross Blevins. He called to let us know that the judge ordered that the interview be completed today."

"Impossible." Lucky didn't even have to think about it. "The driver of that truck might be sitting out there, waiting for round two." He glared at Lois and Howard. They'd no doubt tried to orchestrate scheduling the interview when both Marin and he were not mentally ready.

"I know, and that's what I told the psychologist. But he said the judge insisted. He wants a preliminary report on his desk by close of business today."

Lucky cursed under his breath and intensified the glare at the Sheppards. Lois at least had the decency to look a little uncomfortable. Howard, however, couldn't quite contain his pleasure. To him, this was the next step in regaining control of his daughter.

But that wasn't going to happen.

"I'll call the psychologist," Lucky told her. He hooked his arm around her waist so he could lead her back to the bedroom. "I'll work out all of this."

But Marin didn't budge. "It's too late. Dr. Blevins is already on his way over here to conduct the interview. He should be here any minute."

Chapter Eleven

"Marin was nearly murdered today," she heard Lucky say to Dr. Blevins. Lucky had called the psychologist despite the fact the man was already en route. "The sheriff and his deputy are still here checking out the crime scene. Plus, she just got out of the hospital yesterday."

Marin continued to feed Noah his bottle, and she tried not to react to what was going on around her. Impossible to do. She still had dirt on the knees of her jeans. Dirt she'd gotten from trying to dodge that killer truck.

Lucky's appearance wasn't much better. He had triple the mud and dirt that she did, and unlike her, he was definitely reacting with anger. From what she could judge from the one side of the conversation she could hear, the psychologist wasn't going to postpone the interview.

Apparently aware that she had her attention elsewhere, Noah bucked a little and reached for her face. He pinched her chin, automatically causing Marin to smile.

Looking down at him, seeing that precious little face, was all the reminder she needed that somehow she had to muster enough energy and resolve to get through this ordeal.

"This meeting needs to be rescheduled," Lucky continued. "Marin's attorney hasn't arrived." He paused again. "Yes, I know it's not necessary for her attorney to be there, but we'd like him to be."

Judging from his expression, that didn't go over well with the doctor.

"I couldn't change his mind," Lucky growled a moment later. He jabbed the end-call button and shoved his phone back into his pocket. "He's already here at the ranch and is waiting for us in your father's office."

That didn't surprise her. Her father would want to listen in on the interview, as well. "As soon as I'm finished feeding Noah, we'll go ahead and get this over with."

"Take your time. Let the guy wait." Lucky sat down on the bed beside her and brushed his fingers across Noah's hair. Her son responded with a smile and turned to face Lucky. Noah no longer seemed interested in the bottle and instead reached for Lucky. Marin let her son go into his arms.

"No barfing, okay, buddy?" Lucky teased. He put Noah against his chest and patted his back to burp him.

It was such a simple gesture, something she'd done dozens of times. Still, today it seemed, well, special. Maybe because of the near-death experience. But it also had to do with Lucky. With the way he held her son. The genuine pleasure in his eyes from doing something that many would consider mundane and even a little gross.

"Thank you," Marin heard herself say. Mercy, she was actually tearing up.

Lucky met her gaze over the top of Noah's head. "For what?"

"Everything."

But she immediately regretted that. It sounded gushy. As if she wanted this arrangement to be permanent. She didn't. They were on opposite sides of an important issue: Dexter. Plus, after her ordeal with Randall, she wasn't ready to risk her heart again.

Or Noah's.

Lucky had too much personal baggage of his own to be a real father to Noah.

"The kissing has screwed things up. It gave us this…connection. And it's complicating the heck out of this situation."

Since Marin couldn't deny that and since she had no idea what to say, she figured it was a good time to just sit there and listen.

"If this interview goes well…" Lucky continued a moment later. But he didn't finish it. He didn't have to.

"You'll be leaving the ranch right away," Marin finished for him. "I know. You need to find your sister."

He brushed a kiss on Noah's cheek. "I can't leave until I'm certain you're both safe."

It was tempting to try to keep him there, but she didn't have the right. Or the courage to make a commitment. Besides, he really did need to find his sister. She could be in serious danger. And if she was the person who'd tried to kill them, he might need to stop her from setting another explosive.

"Once the interview is done, I'll leave the ranch, as well," Marin assured him. "I have enough money to hire a bodyguard. Once I'm back in Fort Worth, I'll move again. I'll make sure no one finds Noah and me."

Lucky stared at her. "You can't be sure of that."

"True. But I can't be sure of it if you're with me, either." And then she played her trump card, the one thing that she knew would convince Lucky to leave. "Besides, if Dexter is behind this, Noah and I could be in even more danger just being around you."

It stung to say that, because she didn't believe it was true. She didn't honestly believe Dexter would come after her, even if he was trying to get to Lucky. Still, she needed some leverage to get Lucky to budge in the only direction he should go.

Lucky made an unhappy sound deep within his throat and gave a crisp nod. That was it. No more conversation. No rebuttal of what she'd just said. That nod was all she got before he stood and started for the door.

Marin followed, of course. "We can leave Noah with my grandmother."

He didn't comment on that, either. Lucky merely went down the hall and knocked on her grandmother's door. "Time for the interview," Helen commented, taking Noah from Lucky. "Don't let that head doctor bully you."

Marin assured her that they wouldn't and thanked her grandmother for watching Noah.

The walk down the hall had an ominous feel to it that only got worse when they passed the living room, and saw her parents.

"This is for your own good," her father insisted, again.

"Is it?" Marin fired back, but she didn't give them more than that. She didn't want them to get any satisfaction from seeing her upset. But underneath she was well past being upset.

Dr. Ross Blevins waited in the office. She'd seen him before around town, but had never been introduced. Too bad they had to meet under these circumstances.

Wearing a dark gray suit that was almost the same color as the winter sky and his precisely groomed hair, the doctor stood in front of the bay windows, the sprawling pasture a backdrop behind him. He looked like an inquisitor with his probing blue eyes and judgmental frown.

"Mr. Davidson," the doctor greeted Lucky. It made Marin cringe a little to hear Lucky labeled with the name of Noah's birth father. "Ms. Sheppard. Why don't you two sit so we can get started?"

But Lucky continued to stand, staring at the doctor. "I don't suppose it'd do any good to object to this on the basis that Marin has already been through enough for one day."

Dr. Blevins shook his head and remained perfectly calm. He sat at her father's desk. "This matter should be addressed immediately."

"Why?"

The doctor blinked. Hesitated. "Because the safety of a child is at stake."

"Noah's fine," Lucky insisted. "But this entire witch hunt of which you're obviously a major participant— or a pawn—isn't."

Marin took up the argument from there. "How much are my parents paying you?"

That caused a slight ruffle in his cool composure. A muscle tightened in his jaw. "The county is paying me for what will be an independent, objective assessment. But I have to tell you, you're not off to a good start."

"Neither are you," Lucky fired back.

Dr. Blevins got to his feet. "At least I am who I say I am, *Mr. Davidson.*"

The room went silent, and Marin held her breath because that comment had a heavy punch to it. Coupled with the doctor's now almost smug glare, she knew this was about to take a very ugly turn.

"Sit down," the doctor insisted. He took his own advice and returned to her father's chair. "And then you can explain why you two lied about your relationship."

Marin lost her breath for a moment. Yes, this was an ugly turn. And it would no doubt get even uglier.

Lucky caught on to her hand and eased her into the chair across from where the doctor was seated. Then, he sat, as well, and they stared at the man who could ultimately take Noah away from her.

"You're not engaged," Dr. Blevins continued. "In fact, I suspect you're practically strangers."

"Why do you think that?" Lucky asked. Marin was glad he did. Her throat seemed to have snapped shut.

The doctor propped his elbows on the desk. "Because I know the truth."

"The truth?" Lucky repeated. "I doubt that. What you know is what Marin's parents have told you."

"Her parents didn't tell me. Someone else tipped me

off, and then I did some investigating. I know you're not Randall Davidson. He's been dead for well over a year. I have a copy of his death certificate, though it wasn't easy to get since Randall was his middle name. The certificate was filed as Mitchell R. Davidson."

Since Marin couldn't deny any of this, she just sat there and wondered where this was leading. Would the doctor try to use this to challenge her custodial rights? And if so, how could she stop that from happening?

She glanced at Lucky, and in that brief exchange, she could tell he was as concerned as she was. But there was something else beneath the surface. Resolve. "It'll be okay," he promised in a whisper.

But Marin wasn't sure how anyone could make this okay.

Dr. Blevins stared at Lucky. "Since I know you're not Randall Davidson, would you like to tell me who you really are?"

"Quinn Bacelli." He paused a moment. Leaned forward. And returned the steely stare. "Marin's fiancé."

Marin hoped she didn't look too surprised. But the doctor certainly did. "You're lying."

Lucky shook his head and slid his hand over hers. "Why would I do that?"

"To help Marin keep her son."

"Marin doesn't need my help for that. She's a good mother who's been railroaded by parents who want to control her life." Lucky stabbed an accusing finger at Blevins. "And you're helping them do that."

The doctor shook his head. "I'm trying to get to the truth."

"You have the truth. No, I'm not Noah's biological father, but he's my son in every way that matters."

Lucky sounded sincere. Because he probably was. He did care deeply for her son. But would that be enough to get Dr. Blevins to back off?

"Why did you lie to everyone about who you were?" Blevins asked Lucky.

"Because I asked him to," Marin volunteered before Lucky could answer. "I came to the ranch to visit my grandmother. I wanted the trip to be short. And I didn't want to have to answer what I knew would be a litany of my parents' questions about my personal relationship. I figured it would keep things simple if they thought he was Randall."

The doctor obviously didn't like her quick response. His forehead bunched up, and he was no doubt trying to figure out a way to challenge what she was saying because that's what her parents had told him to do.

Marin pushed harder. "Lucky took care of my son while I was in the hospital. Do you think I'd trust a stranger to do that?" She didn't wait for him to respond. "Do you think I'd have a stranger sleep in my bed?"

"Well?" Lucky challenged when the doctor only stared at them.

"I'll have to tell the judge that you lied about your real identity," Blevins finally said.

"Go ahead. I'll have my attorney contact the judge, as well. And the state attorney general. Because, you see, you might think you're doing the right thing, but I don't believe your motives will hold up under scrutiny from someone who's not beholden to Howard and Lois Sheppard."

The doctor scrawled something on the paper in front of him. "Judge Carrick will get my report today. You should hear something as early as tomorrow."

Marin wasn't sure what that meant, but she had to hope that it would all turn out all right despite this horrible meeting.

She and Lucky stood, but the doctor spoke before they could even take a step.

"Judge Carrick tends to be conservative, even old-fashioned, when it comes to his cases," Blevins said. It sounded as if he were choosing his words carefully. "He wants me to tell you that you're to remain here at the ranch until you hear his decision."

"Lucky has to leave," Marin volunteered. "A family emergency."

The doctor made a sound to indicate he understood. But, of course, there was no way he could. "It could take weeks or even months for someone like the state attorney general to intercede. In the mean time, Judge Carrick could give temporary custody of your son to your parents."

Marin was glad that Lucky still had his arm around her. Still, she didn't want Blevins to see that she was on the verge of losing it. "You can stop that from happening," she told the doctor.

Blevins pulled in a long, weary breath and shook his head. "You were born and raised here, Marin. You know how things work."

That chilled her to the bone. She knew how much power and influence her wealthy parents had. This session had been nothing more than a square filler, the prelude to her parents getting what they wanted—her back under their control.

"I'll help if I can," Dr. Blevins finally conceded. But his tone and demeanor said that his help wouldn't do them any good.

Lucky led her out of the room. "I'll call my lawyer and get her out here."

Marin was so tired from the adrenaline crash and the stress that she nearly gave in. It would be so easy just to put all of this on Lucky's shoulders. But that's what had gotten her in trouble in the first place.

"I'll contact that attorney again in Fort Worth, and while I'm at it, I'll phone my friend Lizette, too. If she's back in town, I know she'll come right away."

Lucky nodded and caught on to her chin to force eye contact. "Are you okay?"

"No. But I will be, after I confront my parents."

"You think that'll help?"

"It'll help me," she insisted. She paused and moved closer so that her mouth was right against Lucky's ear. "I'm thinking about taking Noah and leaving tonight."

He didn't stiffen, nor did he seem surprised. Lucky simply slipped his arm around her and pulled her closer. He brushed a kiss on her cheek. That kiss went through her. Warm lips against cold cheek.

"Your parents won't give up. From the sound of it, neither will this judge. They'll look for you. No matter where you go, they'll keep looking."

"What other choice do I have? I can't let them have Noah. You heard what Dr. Blevins said about temporary custody. It could take me months to sort out everything and get Noah back. In the mean time, I'd be here, right where my parents want me to be."

"There is an alternative, something that might help you keep custody."

"What? I'll do anything." Marin was certain she sounded as desperate as she felt.

Lucky looked her straight in the eyes. "You can marry me."

LUCKY WATCHED HIS marriage proposal register in Marin's eyes. He'd dumbfounded her. She didn't utter a sound. Her mouth dropped open a little, and it stayed in that position while she stared at him.

"It makes sense," he insisted. "If we're married and I make it known that I intend to legally adopt Noah, then how could a judge object?"

But Lucky could think of a reason: Marin's parents were paying the judge so well that the man would find a way around the law. However, a maneuver like that would be temporary at best and highly illegal. Even this judge couldn't be out of reach from the state attorney general or Justice Department. Just like Duran, Lucky intended to use both if it came down to it.

"Marriage?" Marin finally mumbled. "That wasn't something I'd considered."

"I know. We've been in overload mode since we first met." Unfortunately, there were worse things to think about than temporarily losing custody of Noah.

Marin and Noah were in danger.

Marriage wouldn't keep them from a killer, but it would give Marin a little breathing room. He also hoped it wouldn't create a new set of problems. After all, Marin and he were attracted to each other. A marriage of convenience would muddy already murky waters.

She shook her head, but Lucky couldn't tell from her stunned expression exactly what she was thinking. She opened her mouth to answer, but she didn't get to utter a word before his cell phone rang.

"Blocked number," he mumbled, glancing down at the caller ID screen. And he immediately thought of his sister. Was she trying to contact him? "Bacelli," he answered.

But it wasn't his sister's voice he heard.

"Mr. Bacelli, this is Brenna Martel. Your sister and I worked together for Dexter Sheppard."

Well, that was certainly a voice he hadn't expected to hear. But it was welcome.

"I know who you are." He didn't want to put the call on speaker in case Marin's parents were still around, but he motioned for Marin to move closer so she could hear this. "I thought you were dead."

"A lot of people think that."

Of course, Lucky wondered why she was calling and if this call was related to the attempts to kill Marin and him. But right now, he had a more pressing question. "Is Kinley alive?"

Silence. Lucky held his breath. Beside him, Marin was doing the same.

"I'd rather not say anything about Kinley," Brenna finally answered.

"You don't have a choice. I want to know if my sister is alive, and you're going to tell me."

"Not over the phone," Brenna maintained, though her voice was shaky and hardly there. "It isn't safe. The less I say, the safer it will be for me. Someone wants me dead."

"Welcome to the club," Lucky snarled. "Your safety isn't my top priority, so start talking. I want to know if Kinley is alive and if so, where she is."

"No answers over the phone. I want to meet with you and Marin Sheppard."

Lucky didn't bother to suppress a groan. "I'll just bet you do. That way you can get another crack at trying to kill us."

"It isn't me who wants you dead." Despite that whispery, weak voice, Brenna sounded adamant. However, that didn't mean she was telling the truth. Killers were often very convincing liars.

"If not you, then who?" Lucky demanded.

"I don't know. Dexter, maybe. Or someone connected to him. Possibly even Grady Duran. God knows he's furious with everyone right now. I have information, or rather pieces of information, and I don't know how they all fit. That's why I need to see you. We have important things to discuss that involve both of you."

Lucky had to pause a moment to gather his composure. He wanted to know about Kinley, but this sounded a lot like suicide. "You must think Marin and I are fools. Meet with you so you can ambush us?"

"Fool or not, if you want to know about your siblings, you'll see me. Tomorrow morning, 6:00 a.m., at the abandoned drive-in theater. You must arrive together, without the sheriff or anyone else. And if you're carrying a weapon, hold it high so I can see it. Because I don't want to be ambushed, either."

With that, Brenna Martel hung up.

"The drive-in is on the edge of town," Marin immediately supplied, letting him know that she'd managed to hear the conversation. "It's surrounded by a flat field. Last time I saw it, the big screen and the concession stand were still there, but little else. In other words, there aren't many places a person could hide to ambush us."

Lucky was already shaking his head before Marin even finished. "I can't risk taking you out there. Heck, I can't risk taking you out of this house after what happened on our little walk this morning."

She caught on to his shoulders. "You can't miss this meeting, either. Lucky, this could be your best chance to find your sister and for me to know once and for all what happened to Dexter."

He made sure there was plenty of sarcasm in his voice. "You want to meet a potential felon who might have not only faked her own death and stole a chemical weapon, but also tried to kill us twice?"

Marin lifted her shoulder. "What's the alternative? Not ever knowing? Running? Hiding? Brenna Martel might have what we need to stop all of this. She could end the danger so that I can safely get out of here with Noah."

He couldn't argue with that. "Then, I'll go meet with her. I'll hear what she has to say and come back here to tell you."

She cocked her head to the side. "You heard what she said. This meeting will only happen if we're both there."

"Yeah, so it'll be easier for her to kill us."

"Not if we take precautions. I know that drive-in. We used to go there when I was a kid." Marin caught on to his arm when he started to move away. "We can arrive ahead of time, hours before Brenna will be expecting us, and stake out a safe place to wait for her."

Lucky couldn't believe what he was hearing. Or what he was thinking. God, was it even something he should consider?

How could he not?

Judging from the determined look in Marin's eyes, she felt the same. He cursed under his breath. "It's still too dangerous."

"Yes. But you can make it less dangerous. This is what you do. You know ways to minimize the risk."

"Yeah. And you staying here at the house is the best way to do that."

"No." Marin let that hang in the air. "Nowhere is safe until we learn who's trying to kill us. And if it's Brenna, then maybe it's time for a showdown."

"A showdown?" He threw his hands in the air. "With you in the frickin' middle?"

"With us in control of the situation." She pressed her fingers to his mouth to stop more of his protest. "We have to do this, so no more arguing. Instead, let's figure out how we can make this as safe as possible."

He saw it then. The sheer determination on her face. Marin wasn't going to back down from this. Worse? He couldn't let her back down. Because she was right— they had to know the truth.

"I'll set up a safety net. Some security," he said

thinking out loud. "I'll get someone to provide backup so we're not out there alone."

"Does that mean we'll meet her?"

Lucky cursed again. There was really only one answer he could live with. "Yes."

He only hoped that he wasn't leading them straight to their deaths.

"I need to make lots of calls," he explained. "I have a PI friend who can get us some monitoring equipment so that no one can sneak up on us out there."

He would have added more if he hadn't heard footsteps. At first he thought the doctor was coming out of the office, but the footsteps came from the other direction.

Lucky pushed Marin behind him and drew his gun.

Just as Howard and Lois stepped into the hallway.

Lucky didn't put his gun away, and he hoped his glare conveyed his displeasure over what the two were trying to do to their daughter.

"Dr. Blevins just called me on my cell," Howard announced. He kept his attention nailed to Lucky. "He's writing his report now, but he wanted to give us a heads-up about the lie you told. Now, who the hell are you? I know for a fact you're not Randall Davidson."

"Guess there's no such thing as confidentiality when it comes to Blevins," Lucky grumbled. That was something else he could mention to the state attorney general. "My name is Lucky Bacelli."

"Marin, how could you do this?" her mother asked, snapping her attention to her daughter. "You hired this man, this imposter, so that we'd think Noah had a father?"

Lucky spoke before Marin could. "Noah does have a father. *Me.* My feelings for Noah aren't based on DNA. Good thing, too. Because after meeting you guys, I think that whole DNA connection thing is highly over-rated."

Lois stiffened while her husband just stood there and stewed. "Judge Carrick will hear about your lies," she threatened. "You're obviously not thinking straight." She kept her eyes trained on Marin. "If you had been, you wouldn't have brought this imposter into our home. I don't care what he claims his feelings are for Noah. This is a sham of a relationship."

"A sham?" Marin stepped out from behind him and faced her parents. "For the record, Lucky asked me to marry him."

With Brenna's phone call, Lucky had nearly forgotten that. Though it was another critical cog in this complicated wheel they were building.

"You turned him down, of course," her father issued like a warning.

Marin's chin came up. "Actually, I hadn't given an answer yet. But now is as good a time as any." She turned, leaned in and kissed him. A real kiss like the one they'd shared in the closet.

"Yes, Lucky," Marin said. "I'll marry you."

Chapter Twelve

Marin waited, something she seemed to have been doing for hours.

Lucky was on the phone. She only hoped his efforts paid off and that this meeting with Brenna Martel ended with them alive and with crucial answers about Dexter and Kinley.

Lucky had certainly taken every conceivable precaution to assure their safety. It was midnight, a full six hours before the scheduled meeting. They weren't at the drive-in, but rather parked across the field, with their car nestled in some trees. Marin was armed with one of the handguns she'd taken from the ranch. Lucky had his own weapon and a backup that he'd slipped into an ankle holster.

To make sure they were safe and not sitting ducks in the field, Lucky had rigged the area around the car with a motion detector that he'd had delivered to the ranch. With the detector activated, no one would get close enough to ambush them without him finding out.

Lucky had called Dr. Blevins and the judge. There

was no word yet on the outcome of the so-called hearing. No decision about custody. It was a reprieve, but it wouldn't last. Marin needed to make some decisions before the judge made them for her and took her son.

But what were the right decisions?

Lucky was obviously on the same wavelength because in the middle of all this chaos, he'd made wedding plans. Right after announcing to her parents that she'd accepted Lucky's proposal, he'd taken her to town to see the justice of the peace and arranged for a marriage license. And he'd done that without so much as a flicker of emotion. If was as if he'd gone on autopilot.

Get safety equipment. Check.

Call the PI. Check.

Set up security for meeting. Check.

Marry Marin. Check.

It was stupid for that to sting. After all, Lucky was doing her a huge favor by marrying her. Or rather letting her parents *think* he was going to marry her. She wasn't sure he'd actually go through with it. After all, he wouldn't exactly jump at the chance to have a loveless marriage all because he cared for her son.

Marin wondered if there was more to his feelings.

Those kisses had confused her. And they'd made her burn. There was definitely physical attraction there between them. But that would only give her hope about having a real relationship with Lucky, which just wasn't a good idea. The timing was all wrong. She already had too many things to deal with. Lucky did, as well.

"You're positive there's no one around the drive-in?" Lucky asked.

Though Marin couldn't hear the answer, she knew that Lucky was talking to Burney Rickman, a San Antonio PI who had arrived earlier with a carload of security equipment. Lucky had told her that he trusted this man with his life. That was good because even though they had no choice about this meeting, they might need assistance to stay alive.

Thankfully, Noah was back at the ranch with her grandmother and a deputy that Sheriff Jack Whitley had sent over to guard them and the rest of the place. As a backup, her grandmother had an old Smith & Wesson that she definitely knew how to use. Still, Marin was eager to get this meeting over and done so she could get back to Noah, especially since her parents were also at home.

"Burney doesn't see anyone around the drive-in or in the concession stand, and he's searched the entire place," Lucky relayed to her when he finished the call. "He's also using equipment to make sure no one has set up surveillance cameras. If they have, he said it must be low-tech because his equipment's not picking up anything."

"Maybe the meeting is just that. A meeting. Maybe Brenna doesn't have anything up her sleeve." But Marin couldn't trust that. They had to stay vigilant when and if they ever went into that drive-in to talk to her.

It was entirely possible that Brenna wouldn't show.

And if so, they were back to square one.

Lucky's phone rang again, and he immediately glanced down at the caller ID screen. "It's Cal Rico from the Justice Department. I asked him to call if he found out anything about Brenna or Kinley."

Apparently, he had.

"I see," Lucky said to the Justice Department agent a moment later. Lucky sounded puzzled. "But it was my sister's blood on the floor of that research facility."

The comment had Marin moving across the front seat so she could hear what was being said. Unfortunately, the wind didn't cooperate. Winter had decided to return in full force, and the wind was howling right out of the north. Added to that was the sound of the overhead swishing tree limbs, so she didn't catch a word.

Lucky finally pressed the end-call button and slipped the phone back into his jacket pocket. "Cal Rico ran the surveillance disk from the train through some facial recognition software. It was a high percentage match for Kinley."

No wonder Lucky looked so shell-shocked. "You said something about the blood on the floor?"

Because of the full moon, she had no trouble seeing his expression. That call had not been good news. "Cal had the blood from the research lab retested. It belonged to Brenna and Kinley all right, but there was a preservative present. They didn't find the preservatives in the earlier tests because they weren't looking for it."

Marin shook her head. "What does that mean?"

"Someone could have stockpiled their blood, possibly without their knowledge if they thought they were donating to a blood bank. Then the person could have used it to fake their deaths." Lucky paused. "Of course, they could have faked it themselves."

Oh, mercy. That put his sister not only alive, but in the thick of what could be the cover-up to a crime. "It doesn't mean she's behind the attempts to kill us," Marin pointed out. "She could be a pawn in all of this."

Anything was possible, including the prospect that her own brother was the one who was manipulating this situation. Though she didn't want to believe that, Marin had to at least consider the possibility. To do otherwise might be a fatal mistake.

"Just focus on what we can control," Lucky said. But it seemed as if he was trying to convince himself along with her. "Once we know the outcome of this meeting, we'll deal with the individual issues."

"Like the wedding."

Marin hadn't intended to say it aloud. It just sort of popped out of her mouth. And it earned her a puzzled stare from Lucky.

Since the subject was out there, seemingly coiled and ready to strike, and since they appeared to have several hours of free time on their hands, Marin continued. "You know a wedding might not do any good. I mean, my parents will probably just look for another way to challenge me for custody of Noah."

He made a sound that could have meant anything. "You're afraid of marrying me."

She thought about that a moment. "I'm afraid of us."

Lucky had apparently thought about that, too. "Yeah."

Marin thought it best to leave that comment alone. But she didn't. "I can't fall for you."

"Same here."

Surprised at his blatant honesty, she took a deep breath. "Good." They were in agreement.

Then, she made the mistake of looking at him. There he sat, looking hotter than any man had a right to look. He certainly had her number. He could take her mind off anything and move it straight to where it shouldn't be.

Specifically, on having down-and-dirty sex with him. She wasn't exactly the dirty-sex type, but he certainly put some bad ideas in her head. They must have crept into his mind, too, because he cursed. Something sexual and rough.

"I'm thinking about kissing you," he said.

"I'm thinking about it, too," Marin admitted. It was a stupid admission, but he could no doubt see and feel the need inside her.

He gripped the steering wheel. "How much are you thinking about it?"

She noted his white knuckles. His rapid breath. "As much as you are."

He squeezed his eyes shut. Groaned. And when he opened his eyes again, he reached for her.

It wasn't a slow, fluid motion. It was frantic and hungry and totally out of control. Exactly the way that Marin wanted it to be. Their arms tangled around each other, and lowering his head, he placed his mouth solidly on hers.

Lucky nudged her lips apart, though it didn't take

much effort. She was ready to give him everything, even though she knew that wasn't possible here in the car. This car was her safety net. A way of counting to ten. Because Lucky wouldn't let things go too far.

Would he?

The whole forbidden fantasy thing spiked the heat. Lucky was the ultimate forbidden fantasy.

He pushed open her coat and slipped his hand inside to cover her breast. His touch was clever, wonderful, and he somehow managed to caress her nipple through her bra. Coupled with the fiery effects of his mouth, it sent her need soaring.

"We're in the car," she reminded him when he paused long enough for her to catch her breath.

"Yeah. I'm keeping watch."

She opened her eyes to see if he was truly managing to do that. He was. Damn him, he was. Here she was, body on fire, wishing she could strip him naked, and somehow he was kissing her, pinching her nipple *and* keeping watch.

For some reason, that riled her. Or maybe it just made her feel as if she weren't doing her part. "I'll watch," she insisted.

And because of her aroused, ornery mood, she slid her hand down his chest to his stomach. But her wrist brushed against the most aroused part of him.

Lucky sucked in his breath. "You can't do that."

"I'm keeping watch." Oh, it felt so good to say that and see the tormented pleasure on his hot face.

"We can't have sex in this car," he insisted.

"No. We shouldn't even be kissing."

She couldn't argue with that. So, they sat there. Staring at each other.

"Stupid, stupid, stupid," she mumbled. It seemed the threat of danger wasn't enough to cool them down. "Someone could come at us any minute," Marin reminded him.

"The PI would alert us." His mouth inched toward hers again. "And while I'd like nothing more than to be inside you right now, I don't want to have to multitask while we're having sex."

He continued to stare at her. His mouth moved a little closer. His hand slid up her jeans-covered thigh. Her breath stalled in her throat as his fingers touched her.

Marin could have sworn that her jeans dissolved off her. His touch felt that intimate, like breath against skin. She melted, her body preparing itself for more.

Which it wasn't going to get, of course. She repeated that to herself.

"Keep watch a second," Lucky instructed.

Before she could ask why, Lucky pushed her against the inside of the door, lowered his head and replaced his fingers with his mouth.

True, there was denim between his mouth and her sex, but he managed to make her feel ready to climax.

"Keep watch," Lucky repeated.

"I can't see," she warned.

He chuckled, and his warm breath and the vibration of his laughter creating some very interesting ripples in her body.

Lucky made his way back up. Kissed her mouth

again. Then, her cheeks. All the while, he continued surveillance around them.

"This is driving me crazy," she said. "You know that?"

His phone rang, the sound slicing through the car and causing Marin to jump. Just like that, the lightness and the heat between them evaporated. Her heart immediately went into overdrive, and they pulled apart.

Lucky blew out several quick breaths to clear his head, and answered the call, clicking the speaker function. "It's Burney Rickman," the PI said. "A car's headed this way."

Thank God at least one of them was actually keeping an eye on things.

Marin fixed her clothes, tried to fix her brain and peered out into the darkness. "I don't see anything."

"The driver has the car headlights turned off," the PI provided.

In other words, the person didn't want anyone to know she was approaching. Did that mean Brenna had arrived five hours early so she could set a trap for them? Or like them, was she getting a head start to ensure she didn't die tonight? After all, Brenna probably didn't trust them any more than they trusted her.

There was a slight clicking sound. "I have another call," Lucky told the PI. "Stay low. I don't want you spotted." He pressed the button to answer it.

"I know you're here," the caller said. It was a woman.

"Brenna Martel," Lucky supplied to Marin.

"I set up some small surveillance cameras in the surrounding area before I even phoned you for the meeting," Brenna explained. "So, I know what's going on. Who's the big guy with the gun trying to hide in the drive-in?"

Lucky hesitated and looked as if he wanted to curse. "A PI friend. He won't hurt you."

"I'm not willing to take that chance. Tell him to leave now."

"I will if you'll tell me what this meeting is all about."

Now, it was Brenna's turn to hesitate. A moment later, Marin heard another voice. Another woman.

Definitely not Brenna.

"Lucky?" the woman said, her voice little more than a raspy whisper. "It's me. Kinley."

Lucky's sister.

"I need you to do exactly as Brenna says," Kinley warned. "If not, I'm afraid she'll kill us all."

Chapter Thirteen

"Kinley?" Lucky practically shouted into the phone. That was his sister's voice all right—or else a very good imitation. "Is it really you?"

"Yes. You have to tell that man to leave. You have to come now."

He wanted to do just that. But he had to think of Marin and her safety. "How do I know it's really you?"

Lucky heard some whispered chatter between the women on the other end of the line. The woman next to him, however, sat silent and frozen. She was probably as stunned as he was.

"When I was six," the caller said, "you made me a dollhouse out of Popsicle sticks. You painted it lime-green."

Hell. It was Kinley.

Now, the question was, what was he going to do about it?

"We'll be there in a few minutes," Marin said, making the decision for him. His gaze snapped to hers, but she offered no apology. "We have to do this."

They did. But how?

"Sixty seconds," Brenna said, coming back on the line. "Tell your PI friend to get lost and come to the drive-in. Park just beneath the movie screen. Oh, and Bacelli, if you do anything stupid, your sister is the one who'll pay the price."

"Let's go," Marin said the moment that Brenna ended the call.

Lucky tried to push aside all his doubt, but he couldn't. He was taking Marin directly into the line of fire.

"Get in the backseat," he instructed Marin while he called Burney Rickman. "Burney, make it look as if you're leaving. But stay nearby, hidden, just in case I need you."

"Will do."

Lucky started the engine and drove toward the drive-in.

"There's no reason for me to stay in the backseat," Marin insisted. "I have a gun." She took the snub-nosed .38 from her purse. "And I'm not a bad shot."

"Doesn't matter. I don't intend for you to be doing any shooting."

She mumbled some protest, but thankfully did as he said. The backseat wasn't bulletproof, but if something went wrong, she wouldn't be an easy target.

Lucky didn't turn on the car headlights. Though Brenna had him under surveillance, he didn't want to announce his arrival to anyone else. This was a complicated game with a lot of potential players, and what mattered most was surviving this so that he could get Marin and his sister out of there.

He approached the drive-in slowly. Cautiously. On one side was the concession building and projection room. The windows were all shattered. No doors. The concrete-block building was blistered with what was left of flamingo-pink paint.

On the other side of the drive-in was a thirty-foot-wide screen, that had essentially been a white wall, but it was now pocked with baseball-size holes. Moonlight spewed onto the ground, which was littered with metal poles that had once held speakers. Now, though, it looked more like some eerie haunted obstacle course.

Lucky checked his mirror to make sure Marin was staying down and came to a stop where the speaker rows began. He waited, the seconds ticking off in his head.

The phone rang again, and he snatched it up while keeping a vigilant watch on their surroundings. "Drive forward," Brenna instructed. "Stop directly in front of the center of the movie screen."

Of course. The center. The most vulnerable spot. Too vulnerable. And that meant it was time to set some ground rules of his own.

"I have a better idea. You drive forward, too, and meet me halfway. We both stop in the center." He made sure it wasn't a suggestion.

More seconds ticked by. He could hear the rapid jolts of Marin's breath. The wind. The pounding of his own heartbeat in his ears.

"All right," Brenna finally conceded. "But remember, I have your sister."

"And remember that I have something you want or you wouldn't have demanded this meeting."

Though Lucky didn't have a clue what it was that he had. Hopefully, it was something he could use to bargain so he could get his sister and Marin safely out of there.

Brenna ended the call again, and Lucky proceeded to drive forward.

"You think this is a trap?" Marin asked.

"I just don't know." He had a bad feeling, but then it would have been worse if he'd decided not to come.

He spotted the other car. A black two door. It crawled across the grounds toward him, and they stopped at the same time. About ten feet apart.

"Stay put for now," Lucky told Marin. He drew his gun and held it against his leg. After saying a quick prayer that firing wouldn't become necessary, he stepped out of the car, using the door for cover.

A moment later, the door to Brenna's car opened. There was a shuffle of movement, and two women emerged from the driver's side. A tall blond with a sturdy build who dragged the other woman from the vehicle. The other woman, a brunette, was practically frail in comparison, at least six inches shorter and twenty pounds lighter.

Because the brunette had her head hung low, it took him a moment to realize it was indeed Kinley. His sister was there, right in front of him.

And Brenna had a gun pointed at Kinley's head.

His sister had lost some weight, but other than that she looked the same. Short dark brown hair. The Bacelli eyes. One thing was for certain, unless this was some kind of hologram, she was very much alive.

He wanted to go to her. To hug her. To tell her how relieved he was that she was alive. All these months he'd grieved for her and blamed himself for not doing more to save her. But she'd already been saved.

Well, maybe.

After all, Brenna was holding the gun, and it was clear that Kinley was her hostage.

"I'm sorry, Lucky." Kinley was hoarse, and judging from the puffiness around her eyes, she'd been crying.

It took Lucky a moment to find his breath and another moment before he could speak. "What happened to you?"

But Brenna didn't let her answer. "I think Kinley's the one who's been trying to kill me."

Kinley shook her head, her hair swishing against the gun. "No. I didn't try to kill anyone. But someone tried to murder me. Many times."

Lucky wanted to know every detail about what'd happened the last year, but first things first. "Brenna, you need to put down the gun so we can all talk."

"Where's Marin Sheppard?" she asked, obviously ignoring Lucky's request.

He tipped his head to the backseat. "There's no reason to bring her into this. Marin just got out of the hospital, and she's not up to another confrontation."

Brenna jammed the gun harder against Kinley's head. "There are plenty of reasons to bring her into this. Get her out here now, or this meeting is over."

Lucky believed her. Apparently so did Marin because she stepped from the car and lifted her hands in a show of surrender. However, when she joined Lucky behind the door, he could see that she had her gun tucked in the back waist of her jeans. Maybe Marin wouldn't need to use it, but he hated that she was right back in the middle of danger.

"I want to know where Dexter is," Brenna demanded of Marin.

"Is he alive?" Marin demanded right back.

A sound of pure frustration left Brenna's mouth. "I figured you'd be the one person who could tell me that."

"I honestly don't know," Marin assured her. "In fact, I thought all three of you were dead. But now that you're here, I'd like to know if my brother is alive."

"So would we," Kinley agreed. "If he is, he hasn't shown his face. Not to me, anyway. Brenna thought you'd been in contact with him."

Kinley's comment earned her another jab from Brenna's gun, and it took every ounce of Lucky's will-power not to charge at the woman to stop her from further hurting his kid sister. But he couldn't do that. It would put them all at risk. Brenna was obviously on the edge.

"Why don't you put down that weapon," Lucky tried again. "We're all in the same boat here. Someone's tried to kill all of us, and we need to figure out who the enemy is."

Brenna continued to grip the weapon. "Well, it's not me."

"Nor me," Kinley insisted.

"I'm not a killer. I didn't try to run myself down with a truck," Lucky clarified.

Marin glanced at all of them. "I wouldn't have risked

my son's life in a train explosion." Then, she stared at Kinley. "But maybe you did?"

"No!" And Kinley continued to repeat it.

"But you were on the train," Lucky reminded her. God, he hated to do this, to accuse her, especially under these circumstances while she was held at gunpoint. But it had to be done. And if she had endangered Noah and Marin, then heaven help her. Being his sister wouldn't give her immunity from his rage.

"I got on the train because of a note that threatened to kill you. And someone else," she added in a whisper. "But I didn't set those explosives. Once I got on, I checked the suitcase, and it was empty."

"Someone sent you on the train with an empty suitcase?" Marin clarified, though it was more like an accusation.

"Yes," Kinley insisted.

Brenna shook her head. "There's too much missing information from her story. And it just doesn't make sense. A threatening note. An empty suitcase. An explosion, and she comes out of it without a scratch." Brenna spoke in raw anger, but Lucky thought she had a valid point.

"Who threatened to kill me, Kinley?" Lucky wanted to know. But his sister didn't answer. Apparently stunned by his demand and his rough tone, she just stared at him. "Dexter? Who?" Lucky pressed.

His phone rang again. He cursed. It was the worst timing possible. Still, he had to answer it in case something had gone wrong at the ranch.

"It's Rickman," the PI said. "We have a visitor. He

arrived on foot and is coming up on the side of the concession stand. Judging from those pictures you e-mailed me, it's Grady Duran, one of your suspects."

Not just a suspect. The primary one.

"You want me to detain him?" Rickman asked.

Lucky snared Brenna's attention. "Grady Duran is here. You want him to join this meeting so we can get everything out in the open?"

"No," Brenna said at the same moment that Kinley said, "Yes."

"We need to know the truth," Kinley added.

Lucky agreed with her. "Escort him to where we are. Disarm him first, and if he does anything stupid, pound him to dust."

"You can't trust Duran," Brenna said the moment he hung up.

"I can't trust you, either," Lucky reminded her. "Now, while we're waiting, how about an answer to my question. Kinley, who threatened to kill me?"

"I don't know. The threats came by anonymous e-mail."

"And you believed them?" Lucky asked.

Her eyes filled with tears. "I had to believe them. You weren't the only one they threatened. They threatened the child, too."

"Noah?" Marin immediately asked.

"No. *My* child."

Lucky damn sure hadn't expected her to say that.

"She had a baby four months ago," Brenna supplied. "Dexter's baby."

The tears began to spill down his sister's cheeks. "I left him with someone for safekeeping. Someone had been trying to kill me, and the person said he'd go after my son. I couldn't risk it."

Lucky waited a moment, hoping to process all of that. Here he'd just learned his sister was alive, and now there was another child involved in all of this mess?

"And this person threatened to hurt your child if you didn't carry that suitcase onto the train?" Marin asked.

"It's me, Rickman," the PI called out before Kinley could respond. "I've got Grady Duran with me."

Everyone's attention shifted in the direction of his voice. Lucky didn't have any trouble spotting the two men. The bulkier, meaner looking Rickman had a death grip on Duran, but Duran wasn't protesting. In fact, he seemed pleased to be present.

And that made Lucky very uneasy.

Lucky looked at Marin to see what her take was on all of this. Her too-fast breathing said it all. This had turned into a nightmare. But at least it had the potential to put an end to the danger.

"Keep a close watch on Duran," Lucky warned the PI.

"Finally, we're all together," Duran said, sparing each of them a glance before he settled on the gun Brenna was still holding on Kinley. "Either you two have learned how to return from the dead or else you've been hiding because you're guilty of stealing the plans for the chemical weapon. Which is it?"

"I didn't steal anything," Kinley insisted.

Brenna didn't deny it. "Are you the one who's trying to kill all of us?"

But any one of them could have asked the same question.

The corner of Duran's mouth hitched. "If Dexter's behind this, then he must be somewhere nearby laughing his butt off. He gets us all to turn against each other. Or better yet, kill each other. When the dust settles, he'll be the last man standing. And he'll have the plans for my chemical weapon."

"You don't own that weapon," Brenna pointed out.

"I'm the primary shareholder. Or maybe I should say, I'm the one who got stuck holding the proverbial bag when all of you decided to go into hiding." He rammed his thumb against his chest. "I'm the one who'd put up the most money, and I'm the one who had to answer the threatening lawsuits and letters from the silent partner that Dexter conned into investing in this project."

"Silent partner?" Lucky questioned. This was the first he was hearing of this.

As if she'd noticed something, Brenna suddenly jerked her head to the right, toward the old screen. Lucky looked in that direction, as well, though he'd heard nothing other than the wind and the normal sounds of the night.

Hell. Was Dexter about to join them? It didn't sound like footsteps. More like a click. Like the wind catching a piece of that tattered movie screen.

Brenna shook her head. Cursed. She curved her forearm around Kinley's neck and began to maneuver her back toward the car.

Lucky couldn't let them leave. For one thing, Brenna

might truly kill his sister. And for another, he was going to get answers.

"Brenna," he said, trying to soothe her. He stepped away from the meager protection of the car door and inched his way toward the two women. Unfortunately, Marin was right behind him. "Don't leave."

She didn't listen. Brenna shoved Kinley into the car, pushing her into the passenger's seat.

"It's probably just the wind," Lucky let her know, going even closer. "But I'll check it out, just to make sure."

Lucky turned to do that, but before he could shout out the order, he heard another click. At first he thought it was Brenna putting the keys in the ignition because a split second later, her car engine roared on.

But that sound was soon drowned out by the deafening blast to his left.

He had just enough time for his brain to register that it was an explosion. He turned, dove at Marin, trying to get her back into the car.

It was too late.

The explosion ripped through the massive movie screen, and it came tumbling right at them.

MARIN DOVE ACROSS the front seat as a chunk of the screen slammed into the car and missed Lucky by what had to be less than an inch. He scrambled inside, and in the same motion, he started the car just as a massive slab crashed into the windshield.

The safety glass cracked and webbed, but it thankfully stayed in place.

With Duran still in his grip, the PI turned and began to race toward the concession stand.

Lucky shifted the car into reverse, turned to look over his shoulder and hit the accelerator. Even though Marin couldn't see Brenna's car, she heard the woman make her own getaway. But the screen was enormous, stretching across nearly the entire width of the drive-in. It would take a miracle for all six of them to escape without being crushed to death.

"Keep your gun ready," Lucky warned her.

That didn't help steady her heart. Of course, nothing would steady it at this point. It was a terrifying thought to realize that if they made it out of this situation, there might be someone waiting for them. After all, someone had set that explosive.

But who?

Marin took out her gun and waited.

Debris continued to rain down on them. The chunks pelted the car as Lucky maneuvered his way through the obstacle course of metal speaker poles. It seemed to take an eternity, and the seconds clicked by keeping time with the pulse pounding in her ears.

"Take my phone," Lucky instructed. "Call the sheriff. Tell him what happened and that I need him or one of his deputies to meet us at the ranch."

With all the horrible things that could happen zooming through her head, she made the 9-1-1 call and reported the explosion to the sheriff's dispatcher, who assured her that someone would be sent out immediately. Good. It was a crime scene and needed to be secured and examined. Maybe the person responsible had left something incriminating behind.

"Now, look through the recent calls to get the PI's number. Find out if Duran and he made it out," Lucky insisted.

Another lump of the screen smashed into the front windshield, dumping the sheet of broken safety glass onto their laps. With the glass obstruction now gone, she could see Brenna's vehicle on the other side of the drive-in. The roof of her car was bashed in on the passenger's side where Lucky's sister was sitting.

While she located the PI's number, Marin kept her attention pinned to the other car, but she also sheltered her face in case any debris came through what was left of the windshield. A moment later, she watched as Brenna's car disappeared into the darkness. Lucky noticed it, too, and cursed.

"You two okay?" Rickman immediately asked when he answered.

"We're alive." Marin put the call on speaker so that Lucky could hear.

"I want you to go after Brenna," Lucky ordered.

"I'm already on the way to my vehicle," was the PI's answer. "Should I take Duran with me?"

"No. He'll only slow you down, and you can't trust him." Lucky didn't hesitate, either. "By any chance, did you see who set that explosive?"

"I didn't see anyone near that movie screen. But once I catch up with Brenna, I'll check it out." With that, Rickman hung up.

Once they were clear of all the metal poles, Lucky did a doughnut to turn the car around. He slammed on the accelerator again and got them back onto the road.

He slowed when he got to the connecting road, and his gaze darted all around, looking for Brenna's car.

"Are you going after her?" Marin asked. She wrapped her arms around herself to stave off the cold wind that was now gushing through the glassless windshield.

He shifted his posture slightly. "I can't. Too big of a risk." Lucky sped up again.

"Because of me?" But she knew the answer. He didn't want to put her at further risk. Even if that meant not trying to follow Brenna and his sister.

Lucky increased the speed even more, and even in the darkness she could see the troubled look on his face. "We need to get back to the ranch," he said.

That comment chilled her more than the brutal winter wind that was assaulting them. When Lucky had requested that the sheriff or the deputy go to the ranch, she'd thought it was so the person could take their statement. "You don't think this bomber would go to the ranch, do you?"

He glanced at her. Just a glance, but it said volumes. "If this person wants leverage against us, what better way to get it than to go after Noah."

Oh, God. He was right. If this person had no hesitation about blowing up four people, he wouldn't think twice about going after a child.

Marin grabbed the phone to call the ranch, and prayed they weren't too late.

Chapter Fourteen

Lucky had his car door open before he even came to a full stop in front of the Sheppard ranch.

With his gun ready, he hit the ground running. But he didn't have to go far to find proof that everything was okay. Deputy Reyes Medina was right there on the front porch, standing guard.

"Like I told you on the phone," the deputy said, "there's no reason to panic. No one's tried to get anywhere near the house. There are two armed ranch hands out back. Three more are patrolling the grounds on horseback."

"You're sure Noah's okay?" Lucky pressed.

"He's fine," the deputy assured them. "I told Ms. Helen to call me if she heard anything suspicious. Plus, I reset the security system after your mom headed out a little while ago."

That temporarily stopped Marin, who'd already reached the front door. "Where did my mom go?"

"Wouldn't say. But she got a phone call and left not long after you two did."

Maybe that phone call had been from Dexter? Mercy. Was Lois meeting with her son right at this moment? Or was this late night visit somehow connected to the explosion?

"Marin's father didn't go with his wife?" Lucky wanted to know.

The deputy shook his head. "No. He's not here, either. From what I gathered from Ms. Helen, he's been gone for hours."

"Hours?" Marin repeated.

That was troubling, but it didn't overshadow her need to check on her son. She hurried past the deputy, threw open the front door, disarmed the security system and began to run toward her grandmother's room.

Lucky was right behind her.

Her grandmother must have heard the footsteps in the hall because she answered the door after Marin knocked just once and called out her name.

"Noah's safe," Helen said immediately.

But Marin had to see for herself. She rushed across the room and checked the crib Lucky had moved there. He checked Noah, as well, and discovered the little guy was sound asleep. Not that surprising since it was a little after 1:00 a.m.

Marin mumbled a prayer of thanks, lowered the side of the crib, leaned down and lightly kissed Noah's cheek. Lucky couldn't help himself. He did the same, and he felt relief flood through him.

"Let him sleep out the night here," Helen whispered. "No need to wake him."

Lucky agreed, and he was a little surprised when

Marin did, too. That probably had a lot to do with fatigue. She leaned against him, and he felt her practically collapse.

"She needs to rest," her grandmother insisted. "Stress can sometimes trigger a seizure."

Oh, man. Marin didn't need that tonight. He slipped his weapon back into his shoulder holster and scooped Marin into his arms.

"I can walk," Marin insisted.

But he ignored her and headed toward her bedroom. He only got a few steps into the hall when he saw Deputy Medina headed their way.

"Is Marin hurt?" Medina asked.

"No," she answered, trying to wiggle out of his arms, but Lucky held on tight.

"She's exhausted," Lucky explained. "The sheriff will want us to give a statement about what happened at the drive-in, but it's going to have to wait until morning." He didn't ask for permission. Besides, it'd take Sheriff Whitley hours just to process the massive crime scene. "I take it you'll be standing guard all night?"

Medina nodded. "I'll be here until the sheriff says otherwise. The ranch hands, too. I went ahead and reset the security system, and I'll be posted right by the monitor at the front door. That way I can see if anyone tries to open a window or anything."

Lucky thanked the man and carried Marin to her room. He eased her onto the bed, locked the door and took off her shoes.

"No need to treat me like glass," she said, sitting right

back up. "I haven't had a seizure in years. But if you're squeamish about the possibility of it happening, I can go into the sitting room."

Now, that just made him mad. "Squeamish?" he challenged.

He pulled off his boots and practically threw them on the floor. He wasn't much gentler when he removed his slide holster and dropped it onto the nightstand.

She lifted a shoulder and pushed her hair from her face. "We've already been through enough without you having to be on seizure watch."

That also didn't help cool down his anger. "Marin, you might not have noticed, but I'm not here because someone forced me to be here. And hell's bells, I don't want you to have a seizure, but I imagine it'd be a cakewalk compared to what just happened to us."

"Then why exactly are you here?" she snapped. But she immediately waved it off. "What I'm trying to do— and failing at miserably—is giving you an out."

"An out?" There was still a lot of anger in his voice.

She groaned softly and stood. "I think after tonight we both know that Dexter is behind these attempts to kill us."

Lucky shook his head. "How do you figure that?"

Marin gave him a flat look. "He was the only key player not at the meeting. And he was the only one whose life wasn't in danger tonight."

He couldn't argue with the last part, but he sure as hell could argue with the rest of her theory. "So, why would I need an out? If your brother wants us dead, he won't stop just because we're no longer together. Our best bet is to catch the person responsible. And if it turns out to be Dexter, nothing changes. You need my help to keep Noah, remember?"

She looked exhausted, but ready to continue this ridiculous debate. Something Lucky instantly regretted. He'd brought her in here to lessen her stress, not to cause more by arguing with her.

With that reminder, he ditched his own anger, and eased down on the bed next to her. "I'm not treating you like glass. I'm not leaving. I'm not blaming you because of Dexter. And if you have a seizure, I can deal with it. Okay?"

The emotion in her seemed to soften, too, and she sighed and leaned against him. The physical contact was a strong reminder that no matter what the devil was going on, his body always seemed to react to her.

"Now, what about you?" he asked. "How are we going to deal with your concerns?"

She looked up at him just as he looked down at her. "I'll calm down. I won't blame myself because of Dexter. Well, I'll try not to. And I'll continue to try to make you understand that you're not responsible for Noah's safety. Or mine."

The seriousness of the conversation was getting mixed up with all the physical stuff he was feeling for her. Or at least that was the explanation Lucky wanted to believe. He couldn't fall for her. Not with everything ready to crash down around them.

But he was.

"I *am* responsible for your safety," he concluded, causing her to frown.

"Why?"

Good question. He considered dodging the truth but decided against it when he looked into her eyes. He automatically leaned in. "Because I love Noah. And because I want you."

She blinked. "Want?"

He cringed. "Yeah. That shouldn't come as a surprise to you. Not after what happened in the car."

Another blink. "No. Not a surprise. I'm just trying to figure out why your desire…" She stopped. Shook her head. "How *our* desire for each other would make you feel that you need to protect me."

He brushed a kiss on her forehead and hoped he could change the subject with a little humor. "It's a guy thing. You wouldn't understand."

The corner of her mouth lifted. A weary, exhausted half smile. And a damn sexy one at that.

Before he could warn himself to back off from her, which he almost certainly wouldn't heed, his cell phone rang. He fished it from his pocket, glanced at the caller ID and answered it.

"Rickman," he said to the PI. Because he knew Marin would want to hear this, he put the call on speaker phone. "Please tell me you have Brenna and my sister."

"Sorry. I lost them. Or rather, I never found them. By the time I ditched Duran, got to my car and went in pursuit, Brenna and Kinley were gone."

Marin and he cursed at the same time.

"What do you want me to do?" Rickman asked.

Lucky scrubbed his hand over his face. "Go back to the drive-in. The sheriff should be there by now. Try to figure out what the heck happened. If either you or the sheriff find any answers, call me."

"Will do."

"If there's a lull, I also want you to check on what my sister's been doing for the past year," Lucky added. "See if you can confirm if she had a child."

"I'll see what I can do."

When Rickman hung up, Lucky turned his attention back to Marin. No more hot, sexy smile. She looked alarmed again. And stressed. He caught on to her wrist to check her pulse.

"I'm fine," Marin insisted.

He took her pulse anyway and confirmed what he already suspected. "It's been a while since my EMS training at the police academy, but your pulse seems fast to me. Do you have something you can take to make yourself relax?"

"I'm not sure I want to relax."

Lucky understood that. He wouldn't be doing any relaxing, but Marin was a different matter. "Noah is safe, and it'll be hours before he wakes up. Security measures are in place. You're safe, Marin, and rest is the best thing for you."

She nodded, and got up from the bed. She took a prescription bottle of pills from her cosmetic bag on the dresser, popped one of the capsules into her mouth and went into the bathroom to get some water. A moment later, she reappeared. She stopped just short of the bed where he was still sitting and she stared at him.

"What are we going to do, Lucky?" she asked.

Since that sounded like the start of another stressful

conversation, he caught on to her hand and pulled her onto the bed. But since he wasn't totally stupid, he draped the comforter over her so there'd be a barrier between them.

"Get some sleep," he insisted, turning off the light.

He started to move away from her, but she caught on to him and pulled him to her. And in doing so, she revved up his already interested body.

"One," he said, remembering the counting rule. "Two."

Marin pulled him even closer until their mouths were mere inches apart. His breath touched her mouth when he mumbled, "Three. Four."

"Does it help to count?" she asked, her voice like sin and silk.

"Yes," he lied.

Right before he lowered his head and kissed her.

MARIN IMMEDIATELY FELT a sweet tangle of heat in her stomach, and it spread like a wild blaze. Her nipples drew into peaks, the sensitive flesh contracting so that even a brush from Lucky's chest seemed like a thorough, eager caress from a lover's hand. And he kept right on kissing her.

Now, this was the ultimate way to relieve stress.

She didn't hesitate. Didn't give herself time to think. Because if she had, she would have stopped, opting for the more logical approach. But she didn't want logic tonight. She didn't want to think.

She wanted Lucky.

"Are you sure we should be doing this?" he asked with his mouth still against hers.

"I'm sure." She went after his shirt.

He went after hers.

It didn't take much for him to strip her stretchy pullover sweater off her. With his kisses now wild and frantic, he went after the zipper of her jeans while she still fumbled with the buttons on his shirt.

"What about a condom?" He groaned, stopped and stared at her.

"I'm on the pill."

She nearly cheered when she finally managed to open his shirt. And she wasn't disappointed. His body was perfect. All toned and naturally tanned. She gave herself the pleasure of touching him.

Lucky groaned and stripped off her jeans. He slid his hand down her breasts and then her stomach until he reached his goal, working his fingers into the wet entrance to her body. With the skill of an artist, he touched her so perfectly, so intimately that Marin thought she might unravel right in his hand.

Within moments he had her starving for him. What she had been unable to say in words, her body said for her. She wanted more. And she wanted it now. Marin pushed herself against his fingers, trying to relieve the desperate hunger that he had created.

She went after his zipper. Not a simple task. He was already huge and hard, which didn't make it easy for her to free him from his jeans and boxers.

Repositioning her, Lucky removed his hand and pushed himself into the slickly soft heat of her body.

Marin wrapped her legs around him and caught on to his shoulders to bring him even closer. Her body adjusted—no one else had felt this way inside her, no one else belonged inside her.

Marin realized that she had gone a year and a half without a man.

And a lifetime without a lover.

He drove into her. Treating her not like glass, but like a lover that he desperately had to have. Each new stroke, each assault of her mouth with his wildfire kisses became more urgent.

She heard herself moan. Felt herself go right to the edge. She considered trying to pull back, to wait for Lucky. But when she looked into his eyes, she realized, he truly was right there with her.

Marin gave in to the unbearable heat and pleasure.

Lucky did the same.

He kissed her hard and deep as they went over that edge together.

Their breaths were the only sounds in the room, though Marin could feel her heartbeat. And his. It would have been wonderful just to lie there in his arms and let her sated body drift off to sleep. But she wanted to remain alert in case anything else went wrong.

Lucky didn't give into the moment, either. Breaking the intimate contact, he stared down at her. Their limbs were tangled together, their bodies slick with sweat. Marin felt so fragile that she thought she might shatter into a thousand pieces. Nothing could have prepared her for what had happened. Nothing could have been more beautiful, more perfect than what she had just experienced with Lucky.

She relaxed the harsh grip she still had on him, letting

her fingers slide over the tightly corded muscles of his chest. She resisted the urge to ask how he felt about what they had just done. *Was it good for you?* She smiled. Anything she could ask would seem so clichéd, so ordinary.

But surely this couldn't be ordinary.

"Next time, I'll remember to count to ten," he said.

She laughed. A very short-lived moment. She knew he was right—they should have backed off. But she refused to regret this. Especially since this might be the only time they would be together like this.

Lucky moved off her, dropping on the mattress next to her and staring up at the ceiling. Silent. Thankfully, he didn't remind her that this probably hadn't been a good idea.

His phone rang, the sound slicing through the room. Lucky snapped up his jeans, dug his cell from the pocket and glanced at the screen. "The caller's ID is blocked."

The last time that'd happened, the call had been from his sister. Lucky hurriedly answered it and put it on speaker.

But it wasn't his sister this time.

"It's Grady Duran," the caller said. "There's been a murder."

Chapter Fifteen

"Who's been murdered?" Lucky asked. And he held his breath and prayed it wasn't his sister.

"I don't know," Duran insisted. "The sheriff just found a body in the drive-in debris."

Lucky pressed harder for information he wasn't sure he wanted. "Is it Kinley?"

"They haven't identified the body, but it's definitely not Kinley. She's with me."

He felt the relief, followed by a slam of new concern. "How'd that happen?"

"I'd put a GPS device on Brenna's car this afternoon before I ever walked into that drive-in and encountered your PI. I knew Brenna would run if things didn't go her way in this meeting, and she did. When I caught up with them, she pushed Kinley out of the car. I nearly ran over her. And when I stopped to make sure she was okay, Brenna got away."

Oh, man. Lucky did not want to hear this. "Bring Kinley to the ranch," he demanded.

"She's already here. All you have to do is come out and get her."

Marin shook her head and mouthed, "No."

But as dangerous as Duran's offer sounded, Lucky couldn't just dismiss it. "Where are you?"

"In the hay barn on the east side of the pasture. I want you to come here and get your sister."

Lucky cursed. "You mean the same barn where someone nearly ran over Marin and me with a truck?"

"The very one." There was ton of cockiness and danger in his tone.

Before Lucky could even respond, there was another voice. One he recognized. "Duran says to tell you this isn't a trick," Kinley said. "All he wants in exchange for me is information." She hesitated. "Don't come, Lucky." Her voice was frantic, and it sounded as if she were crying. "I don't know if this is a trap—"

There was a shuffling sound. Definitely some frenzied movement. "It's not a trap," Duran said, coming back on the line. "And I'm not giving you a choice. Come now, or I'll make sure you don't see your sister again."

That punched Lucky hard, and he had to force himself not to panic. "What, are you going to kill her?" he calmly asked.

"No, but she'll make a good bargaining chip. You heard what she said. She had Dexter's kid. Dexter hasn't shown any interest in contacting her or the baby, but you never know. He might cave, especially if I remind him how his parents would feel about him casting off his own son. It might shame Dexter into cooperating and coughing up what he owes me."

That would put his sister right in the line of fire. "Kinley's not responsible for what Dexter did."

He hoped.

"Just come," Duran demanded. "We need to get to the bottom of all of this."

Lucky couldn't agree more. "Why should I trust you?"

"For the same reason I have to trust you. Because we have to learn the truth."

He couldn't disagree with that, either. "How will meeting with you accomplish that? According to you, you don't know the truth. Neither do I, and that means this little get-together wouldn't accomplish much."

"There has to be something, some bit of information that we're overlooking. And I'm tired of waiting for it," Duran snapped. "You've got ten minutes. If you're not here, I'm leaving. Oh, and Lucky? Don't alert the deputy or the ranch hands patrolling the place. Because if you do, this *little get-together* will be over before it even starts."

Before Lucky could bargain for more time so he could set up a plan, Duran hung up.

"You're not thinking about going," Marin said. She hurriedly put on her clothes.

While Lucky dressed, he went through his options and realized he didn't have any. Ten minutes wasn't enough time to get the sheriff out there. Of course, he could take the deputy with him, or the ranch hands, but that would leave the house itself vulnerable.

And that might be the real trap.

Duran could be using this meeting to lure Lucky out of the house so that he could get inside.

"If you leave, I'll go with you," Marin insisted. "I can be your backup."

Lucky shook his head, zipped up his jeans and put on his shirt. "You can't. For one thing, it's too dangerous. For another, you just took that sedative, and you're sleepy."

"Not so sleepy that I can't help you."

"You can help me by staying here." Then, he played dirty because the stakes were too high to take her with him. "Think of Noah. You need to be here in case Duran tries to get in the house."

Her breath froze. But there were no more head shakes. She knew he was right.

"I have to hurry," Lucky said, putting on his boots. "I don't think Duran will wait around past that ten-minute time limit he set."

"Then at least let me call the sheriff," Marin pleaded.

"He wouldn't be able to get here in time. Besides, I don't want him to do anything that might spook Duran. Okay?"

She nodded, eventually, though she didn't seem sure of any of this. Neither was Lucky. "I'll be careful," he promised. "I'll approach the barn from behind. I won't let Duran get the drop on me."

Another nod as tears watered her eyes.

"I'm going out the front door," he explained. "So the deputy can reset the security system."

Lucky wanted to give Marin more reassurance, but there wasn't time. The seconds were literally ticking away. So, he kissed her and hoped this wasn't the last time she'd ever see him alive.

MARIN WATCHED FROM the window of the sitting room.

With the curtain lifted just a fraction and with the lights off so that no one could see her, she waited and finally spotted Lucky. He glanced in the direction of the window and hurried toward the meeting with Duran.

She had a very bad feeling about this.

They couldn't trust Duran—this might all be a trap. Even Kinley had thought so. But Marin also understood Lucky's need to try to save his sister. If their positions had been reversed, she would have done the same. She just wished she could have gone with him.

Yawning, she leaned against the window frame and kept her gaze on Lucky until he disappeared into the night. Mercy, why had she taken that stupid sedative? It was clouding her mind at a time when she needed to think clearly about this meeting and the body that'd been found at the drive-in.

Should she call the sheriff?

Lucky had insisted that she not do that, but what if he was ambushed?

He'd need help.

She reached for the phone. Stopped. Rethought the whole argument. And while she was arguing with herself, she saw movement. It was a person walking along the fence, headed in the same direction that Lucky had just gone.

She froze. God, was someone trying to follow him?

Marin searched through the darkness, and when the silhouette stepped from the shadows of some mountain laurels, she saw who it was.

Her mother.

Marin blinked. At first she was certain she was seeing things. But it was indeed her mother. Lois was looking around as if she expected someone to jump out of those bushes.

What the heck was going on?

It was nearly two o'clock in the morning, and it was bitterly cold—hardly the time or the weather for her mother to take a stroll. That meant she was up to something.

But what?

Marin grabbed her coat and the gun she'd taken earlier to the drive-in, and she hurried out of her room toward the front door. "My mother's out there," she said to the deputy. "I need to see what she's doing."

Deputy Medina hesitated. "Lucky said I wasn't to let you leave."

Of course he had. Because he would have suspected that she might try to follow him.

Marin silently cursed. If she didn't get out there, her mother might already be gone, and Marin knew instinctively that something critical was going on. Her mother wouldn't be out there unless it involved her father or Dexter.

"I'll only be a minute, and I won't go far," Marin bargained with the deputy.

He frowned and mumbled his displeasure under his breath. "I'll go with you."

"No." To save further argument, she disarmed the security system. "Stay here. I don't want my son and grandmother left alone."

Marin hurried out before the deputy could stop her, and ran across the front lawn to get to the side of the house. Thankfully, the moonlight cooperated. She saw her mother on the trail just ahead.

Marin shook her head to fight off the dizziness from the sedative. Just in case, she kept her gun ready.

"Mother?" she called out, trying to keep her voice low. They were still far enough away from the barn that Duran shouldn't be able to hear them, but Marin didn't want to take any chances.

Her mother stopped and turned. "No," she whispered. Her warm breath blended with the frigid air and created a wispy surreal haze around her. "You shouldn't be here."

"Neither should you. What are you doing out here anyway?" Marin asked.

"Taking a walk."

It wasn't a convincing lie, and coupled with the troubled look on her mother's face, Marin knew that something was terribly wrong.

"Why don't you come back inside," Marin suggested. "I'll make you a cup of tea. We can talk."

Lois frantically shook her head. "I'm too antsy for tea. I need to walk. But you look exhausted. Go back to your room, Marin. I meant what I said—you shouldn't be out here."

That sounded like a warning.

Marin didn't want to bring up Lucky and the meeting with Duran, so she took a different approach in the hope of learning what was going on. "Mother, is Dexter alive? Are you about to meet with him?"

She dodged Marin's stare. "I don't know if he's alive."

"You're lying again."

Lois looked around. Her breath was too fast. Her eyes, almost wild now. "You'll turn him in to the police."

Marin felt everything inside her go still. "Dexter's really alive?"

Her mother nodded and then groaned. "He didn't want you to know. He said you'd go to the police."

And she would have. Marin couldn't deny that. Her brother had put her son in danger, and Noah's safety came ahead of her brother's desire to go unpunished for the things he'd done wrong.

"He faked his death?" Marin asked.

Lois hesitated so long that Marin wasn't sure the woman would answer. But she finally did. "He faked his death, Brenna's and Kinley's."

"Kinley had his child."

Her mother's eyes widened. Her reaction was too genuine for it to be fake. "He didn't tell me that. He's been in Mexico. The people who invested in his project wanted to kill him."

That was not good to hear. Marin glanced back at the house to make sure it looked safe and secure. Thankfully, it did.

"But the investors are dead now," Lois continued. "Dexter took care of them."

Oh, mercy. "He killed them?"

"He had to. Don't you see? If he hadn't, they would have killed him. And he could have never come home."

That tightened the knot in her stomach. "But he's home now?"

Lois smiled and touched Marin's arm. "He's home," she said with all the joy of a mother who was about to see her son. Marin could understand that on some level—she had a son. But unlike her son, Dexter was a killer. "He called this afternoon to tell us that he was back. Soon, we'll all be a family again."

Not a chance. Dexter would know that she wouldn't want him anywhere near Noah.

Then, it hit her. "Lucky," Marin whispered under her breath.

God, was Dexter going after him? Did he plan to eliminate Lucky, too?

Blinking back another wave of dizziness, Marin considered running toward the barn. Maybe Dexter was there, waiting to ambush Lucky.

Her mother stiffened and whirled around to face the other direction. The direction of the barn. Her gaze flew to her watch and the lighted dial. "I have to go. It's time."

Marin caught on to her arm. "Time for what?"

"To meet Dexter. He should be waiting in the truck that I left for him at the hay barn. But you can't come. If he sees you, he'll leave." Lois began to run, staying on the trail.

Marin considered following her directly. But that would be a dangerous move, especially if Dexter wanted her dead. Instead, she waited several seconds until her mother had a head start, then went off the trail, using the mountain laurels for cover. She slapped aside the low hanging branches and began to run. She'd get to the barn taking the same path that Lucky had likely taken.

She prayed she wasn't too late to save him from her brother.

Chapter Sixteen

Lucky eased his way through the darkness and the meager shrubs. There wasn't a lot of cover once he got close to the barn.

He was a sitting duck.

And there wasn't much he could do about it.

He kept telling himself that if Duran wanted to kill Kinley, he would have already done it. So, now the trick was to get to this meeting and come up with some kind of resolution that would set his sister free.

A twig snapped beneath his boot, spiking his heartbeat and causing his finger to tense on the trigger of his gun. Lucky paused, waiting to make sure the twig hadn't alerted anyone. It apparently hadn't. He continued forward one cautious step at a time.

There was no light on in the barn, but the entire structure was visible because of the watery white moonlight. The wind was still stirring and that made it next to impossible to know if he was about to be ambushed.

He saw a truck parked at the back of the barn. It wasn't the same one that'd been used to try to kill him, but he was certain he'd seen the vehicle on the ranch.

Lucky walked toward it, keeping vigilant. He wanted to be sure he was mentally and physically ready for whatever was about to happen.

When he was within twenty feet of the barn, he picked up the pace. He practically ran until he got to the north side of the structure, and then to the passenger's side of the truck. He paused there and listened for any sound to indicate something was wrong.

Everything was quiet.

Too quiet.

He glanced inside the truck. It was empty. No keys in the ignition. There was no one in the back, either. Which meant the person who'd driven it, Grady Duran probably, was already inside the barn. If Duran had truly been the one who'd tried to run them down, then Lucky intended to make the man pay.

Trying not to make his presence known, he maneuvered his way to the back entrance, a double set of high wooden doors, one of which was slightly ajar. He peeked in, but it was too dark to see anything.

He stepped inside.

The toe of his left boot rammed into something soft and pliable that didn't budge when Lucky gave it a light shove with his foot.

He waited a moment, until his eyes could adjust to the darkness. Lucky saw the bales of hay stacked on both sides of the barn in staggered piles. They seemed to extend to the ceiling, and there was only a narrow path that cut through the middle of the barn.

And then he looked down.

What he'd walked into was no bale of hay.

It was a body.

"Hell," he cursed.

Without taking his attention off his surroundings, he stooped and fumbled around until he located the person's neck. He shoved his fingers against the carotid artery.

Nothing.

Not even the hint of a pulse.

Frantic now, he prayed this wasn't his sister. He turned over the body. Not Kinley.

Grady Duran.

There was blood. Lots of it. It spread out across the entire front of Duran's shirt.

Both the blood and the body were still warm.

That just had time to register in his head when he heard a muffled scream. But it wasn't so muffled that he couldn't figure out who'd made that blood-chilling sound. Kinley. He was certain of it.

With his gun ready and aimed, he stepped over Duran and began to make his way through the maze of hay bales. He had to find his sister. She was in trouble. The person who'd killed Duran might have already gotten to her.

There was another sound.

Lois Sheppard.

And Marin.

He couldn't understand exactly what Marin was saying, but she sounded close, probably just outside the barn. His first instinct was to shout for her to stay back.

To tell her to run. To get away. But he didn't have time for that.

Then pain exploded in his head.

Lucky felt himself falling, but there was nothing he could do to stop it. He hit the hay-strewn floor of the barn hard just as the world went blank.

His last coherent thought was that he wouldn't be able to save Marin.

"DEXTER?" LOIS CALLED out again.

Marin caught up with her mother just outside the barn and tried to stop her from shouting Dexter's name.

"This could be dangerous," Marin warned. There were no signs of Lucky. Nor his sister or Grady Duran.

Not Dexter, either.

No signs of anyone. A meeting should be taking place, but where were all the parties? Where was Lucky?

"Dexter's in there," her mother said, and she bolted for the barn.

Since it was obvious her mother wasn't going to stop her quest to see Dexter, Marin got her gun ready and followed her through the front entrance. The place was pitch-black. She reached for the overhead light, only to realize that wasn't a good idea. She grabbed a flashlight from the tack shelf instead and turned it on.

She fanned the circle of light over the darkness, and the first thing she saw was Kinley.

Lucky's sister was tied to a post, gagged and blindfolded with rags. She was struggling to get free and mumbling something.

And that's when Marin noticed Lucky.

Lying on the floor.

"Lucky?" Even though it occurred to her head that it might be a trap, she couldn't stop herself from running to him. God, he couldn't be dead.

He wasn't moving.

Her panic soared when she saw blood on his head. Not a gunshot wound. At least she didn't think it was. The wound was small, and he wasn't gushing blood. It looked as if someone had clubbed him across the back on the head.

"Lucky?" she repeated.

With the gun in her right hand and the flashlight in her left, she stooped down, rolled him onto his side and made sure he was breathing.

He was.

Thank God. But he still needed medical attention. She reached for her cell phone, only to realize she'd left it in her room.

"Mother, do you have your phone with you? I need you to call for help."

Her mother didn't answer. She looked behind her, turned the flashlight in that direction and saw nothing.

Her mother was gone.

Marin got up to run to Kinley, to see if the woman had a phone, but then she felt something.

Lucky gripped on to her arm. "You need to get out of here," he warned, forcing his eyes to open. He winced in pain and touched his fingers to his injured head.

Despite his weak voice, she felt relief. He could speak. However that didn't mean he didn't have serious injuries. "I need to get you to the hospital. You're hurt."

Lucky shook his head. "You have to leave. *Now.* Duran's dead."

An icy chill went through her. "Dead, how?"

"Shot."

Mercy. Was Dexter responsible? Probably. But she didn't have time to point fingers now. "Can you stand up? I have to get you to the hospital. Kinley, too."

"Where's Kinley?" He sat up and wobbled, so Marin helped him to his feet. Somehow. She cursed her own dizziness and weak legs.

"She's here in the barn. Alive." Marin hadn't seen any obvious injuries, but that didn't mean there weren't some.

And where the heck was her mother?

With Lucky leaning against her and with her gun clutched in a death grip, they made it through the hay bales to the front of the barn.

The moment Lucky saw his sister, he reached for her, and though he was clumsy from his injury, he pulled the gag from her mouth.

"Watch out!" Kinley immediately shouted.

From the corner of her eye, Marin saw the movement. And the gun. It was aimed right at Lucky.

"No!" she yelled and automatically turned the flashlight and her gun in the direction of the shooter.

White light slashed across the barn like a razor, blinding the shooter. That didn't stop him from shooting.

Kinley screamed.

But it took Marin a second to realize the bullet had missed her and that it had smacked into a hay bale on the other side of the barn. Bits of dried grass burst into the air.

Praying that the dizziness from the sedative would go away, Marin readjusted her aim and braced herself to return fire. And then she saw the shooter.

Her father.

He re-aimed and pointed his gun right at Lucky.

Marin didn't think about the situation or anything else. She just reacted. She dove in front of Lucky, just as he tried to pull her behind him. They collided, both ending up right in the line of fire.

"Get out of the way, Marin!" her father ordered.

There was no chance of that. In fact, she moved back in front of Lucky. Well, as much as Lucky would allow her to do.

"Dad, what are you doing?" she shouted.

"Saving you. You need to get out of here." His gaze was frozen on Lucky. And Marin knew in that moment what her father was doing.

He intended to kill Lucky.

"Did you murder Duran?" Lucky asked her father.

Howard moved to the side, obviously trying to position himself for a better shot. He had a set of keys hooked to his belt that jangled when he moved.

Marin didn't believe her father would kill her to get to Lucky. But she couldn't be sure. She couldn't be sure of anything right now. Her world had just tipped upside down.

"I had to get rid of him. He got in the way."

Oh, God.

Her father was a killer.

"You've gotten in the way, too," Howard continued, aiming his comments and his gun at Lucky. "And like Duran, you're getting too close to finding out the truth about Dexter."

Blinking back tears and trying to deal with the horrific image of her father as a cold-blooded murderer, Marin moved, intending to use herself as a shield.

"And what truth would that be?" she asked.

"That Dexter's alive," Kinley provided. That hung in the air for several seconds. "Howard helped him fake our deaths that night in the research lab because Dexter took money from the wrong people. Not just from Duran, but from other investors. Dexter promised both he'd deliver a weapon I learned that we couldn't deliver. We only had the technology for components of the weapon, not the entire package."

"So, Duran and the other investor were going to get their money back any way they could," Howard supplied. "One of them put a contract on Dexter's life. That's when I knew I had to help my son."

"You helped him by blackmailing me into staying quiet," Kinley fired back. She looked at Lucky. "I'm so sorry."

Lucky glanced at her, but like Marin, he kept his attention on Howard.

And on his trigger finger.

"Now that Duran's dead and I've discovered the identity of the other investor who's after Dexter," Howard continued, "the only thing I need to clear up is this mess." He tipped his head first to Kinley and then to Lucky.

"You aren't going to try to kill them," Marin insisted.

"I won't try. I'll *succeed*. I have to, for Dexter's sake." Turning to the side so he could still keep an eye on them, her father pulled the barn door shut and, with his left hand, used the key on his belt to lock them in. Of course, the back entrance was still open. If possible, they could use that way to escape.

Because she had no choice, Marin tried again. She had to make her father see that what he was doing was crazy. "You'll be arrested. You'll go to jail for murder."

"No. Brenna will take the blame for this. She has to be eliminated, too. After I'm done here, I'll find her and plant this gun on her."

Lucky inched closer to her father. "The deputy's at the house. You plan to kill him, too?"

"No. He won't hear a thing," he said, waving the silencer at Lucky. "Neither will the ranch hands that I asked to patrol the place. I told them to stick to the front of the ranch. They won't come back here."

Mercy. He had planned all of this. She had to do something to stop him. It would have been easier if he were ranting and out of control. Then, maybe she wouldn't have seen the small part of her father that still remained.

"Why would you risk killing your own daughter?" Marin asked.

He looked genuinely insulted. "I don't want to hurt you. I'm only doing what I have to do to save your brother."

"But you nearly killed Marin and Noah on the train

and then again at the drive-in," Lucky pointed out. He took another step closer.

"I didn't set those explosives. Dexter did. And even though I was furious when I learned what he did, I forgave him because he was desperate. *I'm desperate.*"

Marin didn't doubt that. She could see the pain etched in his face. That meant she might be able to talk him out of this insanity.

"And what about Mother? Is she in on this with you, too?" Marin asked, wondering if her entire family had gone stark raving mad. She also wanted to keep her father occupied so that maybe he wouldn't notice that Lucky was maneuvering himself closer.

"Not a chance. Your mother has no idea. That's why I sent her back to the house. I told her that Dexter would meet her there. That's the plan, anyway."

With his gun still aimed right at Lucky, her father walked closer and latched on to her arm. "I don't want you to see this. It might trigger a seizure."

She wanted to laugh at the irony. Her father didn't want to trigger a seizure, but he was willing to kill the man she loved.

In that moment, Marin realized that she loved Lucky. Talk about lousy timing.

"I can't let you do this," Marin said.

But before the last word left her mouth, her father reached out, lightning fast. With a fierce grip, he knocked the gun from her hand. Lucky bolted forward, but her father turned his gun in Kinley's direction.

"Back off," Howard warned.

Lucky froze and stared at Marin. She could see him

process their situation. He couldn't risk killing his sister, or getting himself killed. Because every minute he stayed alive was another minute he had to get them all out of there.

Only then her father latched on to her and started dragging her toward the back exit of the barn, away from Lucky.

Chapter Seventeen

For Lucky, this was a nightmare.

Marin's father was ready to kill him and Kinley, and now Howard was literally dragging Marin away from the crime scene. God knows what the man would do to her when she didn't cooperate with his plan to protect Dexter.

And Marin wouldn't cooperate.

Lucky was certain that it was that lack of cooperation that would get her killed. Because despite Howard's assurance that he wouldn't hurt her, the man would obviously do anything to protect his precious son. Lucky understood that on some level. He loved Noah and would protect him. But not like this.

"Stop," Lucky warned Howard, and he stepped toward the man cautiously. Lucky didn't want Marin's father accidentally firing that gun and hitting her.

But Howard didn't stop.

Marin didn't stop struggling, either.

"Don't come any closer," Howard threatened Lucky. "You and your sister better stay put, or Marin will pay the price. I'll kill her if you try to escape."

Marin dug in her heels and punched at him, trying to knock the gun from his hand. Cursing, Howard finally gave up and pushed her at Lucky. The impact sent them both crashing into a wooden post.

Howard aimed his gun again, this time at Marin.

"Put down your weapon," Howard warned him, "or I'll shoot her."

Lucky wanted to believe it was a bluff, but he could tell from the stony look in Howard's eyes that it wasn't. Howard had chosen which child to protect.

It wasn't Marin.

"You're doing this for nothing," Lucky insisted.

"Put down the gun," Howard repeated. He took a step closer to them. At this distance, he wouldn't miss, and the shot would be fatal.

Lucky dropped his gun onto the floor and inched himself in front of Marin and Kinley. "Dexter is dead." It was a bluff. A calculated one.

Howard shook his head and stepped even closer. "You're lying."

"No. I'm not. A little while ago Sheriff Whitley found a body at the drive-in. It's Dexter. He died when he set the explosions to kill us."

Marin's father froze.

"Think about it," Lucky continued, hoping that if this was a bluff, it'd stand up to scrutiny. "You haven't heard from Dexter since the explosion, have you?"

"That doesn't mean he's dead."

No, it didn't. But Lucky had put enough doubts in Howard's head. With his hand shaking, Howard unclipped his cell phone from his belt and pressed a button.

The seconds crawled by.

Because the barn had gone deadly silent, Lucky could hear the rings to Dexter's number. No one answered.

Howard's concern kicked up considerably, and while volleying nervous glances between them, he pressed in another set of numbers, looking for someone who could verify Dexter's whereabouts.

Just in case Dexter happened to be alive, Lucky got ready to launch himself at Howard. It would be a risk, of course, but doing nothing would be even a bigger risk. Even if Howard changed his mind about killing Marin, there was no chance he'd let him and Kinley go.

Lucky kept a close watch on Howard's body language while he waited for an opportunity to strike. He glanced at Marin and hopefully conveyed that when the time came, he wanted her to get down.

Marin shook her head, just a little, but enough to let him know that she wasn't going to let him do this alone.

Hell.

"Think of Noah," he mouthed. "He needs you."

It was the second time tonight he'd used the little boy to get her to cooperate, but if this was the only way to save her life, then Lucky didn't feel the least bit guilty. He wanted Noah's mom alive so she could raise him.

"Sheriff Whitley," Howard said when the person on the other end of the line answered the call. "Tell me about the body you found at the drive-in."

Lucky shut out everything else but Howard Sheppard. He watched his face, and Lucky knew the exact moment that the sheriff confirmed exactly whose body had been found.

A hoarse sob tore from Howard's throat. A wounded, helpless sound. But Lucky didn't let it distract him. Nor did he let it allow him any sympathy for the man who'd been about to kill them all.

He launched himself at Howard, plowing into him with full force and knocking him to the ground. Howard's phone went flying.

His gun didn't.

Howard somehow managed to keep a firm grip on it. He could fire at any second, and the bullet could hit Marin or Kinley.

"Get out here now, Sheriff!" Lucky shouted so that Whitley would hear him.

Lucky heard Marin move, first to recover her gun, and then to join the battle. Not good. He wanted her far away from this, but Marin obviously wouldn't have that. She pushed at her father, trying to force them apart.

Howard threw out his hand, and the gun. Lucky was certain he lost ten years of his life when he saw the barrel aimed at Marin.

"Get down," Lucky yelled.

The imminent threat gave him the extra jolt of adrenaline he needed. Despite being bashed in the head, Lucky gathered every ounce of strength he had, grabbed on to Howard's right wrist and slammed his hand against the barn floor. It took three hard jolts.

Then, the gun skittered across the floor.

Lucky didn't waste any time. He drew back his fist and landed a punch to Howard's jaw. Howard stopped moving, stopped fighting.

He surrendered.

"Make sure the sheriff is on his way out here," Lucky instructed Marin. He grabbed Howard by his shoulders and flipped the man onto his stomach. "And then untie Kinley so I can use those ropes."

He didn't want to risk Howard having second thoughts and trying to come at them again. Lucky didn't want to have to shoot the man, especially not in front of Marin.

With the cell phone sandwiched between her shoulder and her ear, Marin worked frantically to set Kinley free. Once Marin had her unbound, she tossed him the rope. Lucky reached up to catch it when he heard something.

He whirled around toward the sound. It'd come from the back of the barn, from the path he'd taken between the stacks of hay.

Someone was there in the darkness, directly behind Marin. Because she was still working to free his sister's feet, she probably hadn't heard the sound or noticed the other person.

Lucky aimed his gun at the newcomer and tried to make sure Howard didn't get free. He was obviously having second thoughts about his surrender because he began to struggle.

"Marin," Lucky warned. "Watch out."

She, too, spun around, just as their visitor stepped from the shadows. The illumination from the flashlight was more than enough for him to recognize the person.

Brenna Martel.

She had a gun clutched in her right hand, which she held just beneath a bulky blanket.

Lucky's heart dropped to his knees when he saw what Brenna had in that blanket.

Noah.

MARIN FELT THE SCREAM rise in her throat.

Her son wasn't moving.

Noah was just lying there bundled in the blanket in Brenna's arms. It took Marin several terrifying seconds to realize that he was asleep, that Brenna hadn't hurt him.

Both Lucky and Marin bolted toward Brenna, but Brenna merely raised her gun. "I wouldn't do that," she warned, her voice hardly louder than a whisper. It didn't need to be any louder for them to understand that Brenna meant business.

And that she had the ultimate bargaining tool.

"Give me Noah," Lucky insisted.

Marin tried to demand the same, but her mouth was suddenly so dry that she couldn't speak.

Her father, however, had no trouble responding to the situation. Without Lucky bearing down on him, he got up from the floor.

Brenna shifted the gun in Howard's direction. "You're not going anywhere. Back on the floor. While you're at it, I want the key to the front door."

Her father actually looked ready to argue, and that infuriated Marin. And terrified her.

"Do as she says," Lucky warned Howard, giving him a chilling glare that seemed much more threatening than Brenna's gun.

Mumbling something under his breath, her father

tossed the keys in Brenna's direction. They landed, clanging, just at her feet.

Howard sat back on the floor. He'd be able to strike easily from this position. If he'd been on their side, Marin wouldn't have minded that, but she had no idea what her father would do if cornered.

"Did you hurt my grandmother?" Marin asked Brenna.

"No." Brenna picked up the key, slipped it into her pocket and checked her watch. "I didn't hurt anyone, not even the police officer guarding the place. I covered my face with a stocking cap so he wouldn't see who I was and then sneaked up on him and held him at gunpoint. I tied him up after I forced him to disengage the security system. I found your grandmother, tied her up and took Noah."

Marin wasn't sure she could believe her, but she held onto the possibility that her grandmother was safe. She had to be alive and well.

"Please," Marin said to Brenna, "give me my son."

"I won't harm him," Brenna promised though she didn't seem convincing. Actually, she seemed disoriented. Her eyes were red and puffy. "I just wanted him here to make sure you would cooperate."

Oh, she'd cooperate, all right. First chance she got, she would get Noah away from this woman.

"Dexter's dead," Brenna whispered a moment later.

"Yes," Marin confirmed. "I think he died while trying to kill us." This wasn't a conversation she wanted to have right now. All she wanted to do was run to her son and get him out of Brenna's arms.

Brenna shook head. Then, the tears welled up in her

eyes. "Dexter didn't mean to hurt me." Just as quickly though, she blinked those tears away and shot Howard a look that could kill. "But you wanted to hurt me. You were going to murder Kinley, Marin and Lucky and set me up to take the fall. Thanks a lot, you miserable piece of slime."

Howard didn't deny it. In fact, he seemed defiant.

"I can't let any of you live," Brenna continued. She glanced at Howard. "Especially you." And then another glance at Kinley. "And you."

"Kinley has nothing to do with this," Lucky insisted.

"She has everything to do with it. Dexter slept with her. He cheated on me——"

"He broke things off with you," Kinley volunteered. "I would have never gotten involved with him while he was still with you."

The pain and tears in Brenna's eyes instantly went away, and in their place was raw anger. Marin had already been terrified for her son, but that look took her beyond that. It took every ounce of her willpower not to launch herself at Brenna.

"Don't," she heard Lucky say. Obviously, he knew what she was thinking. He had the same need to protect Noah.

"So, what are you going to do?" Howard snarled.

"I'm leaving."

"Leaving?" he questioned. "And what makes you think I won't come after you?"

"Noah," Brenna answered without a shred of doubt in her voice. "He lives if all of you stay put. It's as simple as that."

Mercy. Brenna would use Noah to save herself.

"You mean if we stay put and die?" Howard countered.

"I mean if you're willing to sacrifice yourself for the life of a baby. For your grandson," Brenna added. She looked at Kinley. "Your death will be quick. Painless. Because in five minutes or so, this place will be a fireball. That'll happen with or without Noah here inside. Your decision."

"Oh, God." Marin pressed her fingers to her mouth and tried to figure out how to get away from this. "Please don't hurt Noah."

"Don't worry," Brenna said almost calmly. "I'll make sure he's raised by a good family."

And with that, she started to back out of the barn.

"You don't have to do this," Lucky said.

He took a step toward her, but Brenna lifted her gun. She didn't quite aim it at Noah, but she sure as heck implied that's what she would do.

"I do," Brenna said, spearing Howard's gaze. "Don't I?"

"What does she mean?" Marin demanded when her father didn't say anything.

"I'm a wanted woman, thanks to your dear ol' dad. The man I love is dead. I'm flat broke. I don't even have the components to the chemical weapon that I helped create. Why? Because Dexter sold them on the black market to make some money, and when he did that, he leaked my identity to Howard."

"Brenna Martel is the other investor that the Feds are looking for," Howard supplied. "She used every penny of a trust fund her grandmother set up for her." That helped put the puzzle pieces together.

Brenna continued, "I'll be wanted for murder of the security guard who was killed in the explosion at the research facility once the authorities find out I'm the one who actually set the explosives. I'll be looking at the death penalty."

So Brenna had nothing to lose.

"Without money, where will you go?" Marin hoped it would make Brenna rethink this lethal plan.

"Somewhere I can start fresh." Brenna took another step back. It wouldn't be long before she was out that door. With Noah as a hostage, there was no way Lucky could stop her with his gun.

Plus, seconds were ticking away. It wouldn't be long before the explosives went off. And as much as Marin wanted to live, she didn't want her son anywhere near the place if it blew up.

"Wait," Lucky said to Marin. "Let everyone leave. Give Noah to Marin. I'll go with you. I'll be your hostage. And everyone here will be sworn to secrecy. No one will know you're the investor. I'll use my contacts in the Justice Department to help you clear your name."

But that didn't stop Brenna. She continued to move back. Faster now. While volleying her attention between them and her watch.

How much time did they have? A minute, maybe two? Was that enough time to get Noah from Brenna and save themselves?

Marin didn't think so.

Knowing she had to do something, fast, Marin

glanced at Lucky. He looked at her at the same moment. A dozen things passed between them, and with that look, he promised her that he would save her son.

Even if it cost them their lives.

Marin nodded. And braced herself to do whatever it took to get Noah to safety.

A deep growl came from Lucky's throat. It was the only warning she got before he charged at Brenna. The woman had just glanced at her watch again. It took her several seconds to re-aim her gun. She managed to do that, just as Lucky got to her and wrenched Noah from her arms.

Marin was right there, behind him, ready to take her son.

"Run!" Lucky yelled.

Noah yelled, too. The sudden movement and the shout woke him up, and he began to cry. His screams blended with the sound of the struggle.

Somehow, Marin made it past Lucky and Brenna, though their arms and legs seemed to be blocking every inch of the narrow path between the stacked hay bales.

Marin wanted to help Lucky. She wanted to help him get that gun from Brenna. But it was too huge of a risk to take. She had to get Noah out of there.

So, she ran. Just as she reached the back door of the barn, a shot rang out.

Chapter Eighteen

Lucky ignored the deafening blast from the shot that Brenna fired. He wasn't sure, but he thought it'd landed in the barn loft. He had Brenna's right hand in a death grip and had purposely turned the weapon upward in case she fired.

Which she did.

Lucky ignored the shot so he could keep up the fight to gain control of the weapon. But Marin, Noah and his sister still weren't safe. Worse, Howard might use this particular battle to subdue Kinley so he could use her as a bargaining chip. But there'd be nothing to bargain for if those explosives went off.

"Get out," Lucky shouted to his sister.

From the corner of his eye, he saw Kinley try to do exactly that. Howard, too. Marin's father charged at them while he was still trying to free himself from the ropes that Lucky hadn't had time to secure tightly enough.

Lucky bashed Brenna's hand against one of the posts, and the impact dislodged the gun from her grip.

He pinned her against the hay long enough for Kinley to get by. His sister went running to the back exit.

With Brenna in tow, Lucky grabbed her gun and followed his sister.

Behind him, he heard Howard, and Lucky tried to keep watch to make sure the man didn't ambush him. But thankfully, Howard must have realized they were in dire straits because he was as eager to get out of the barn as Lucky was.

Brenna, however, was a different matter. She continued to fight, scratching at him, while he maneuvered her through the hay. Once he reached the exit, he latched on to her and started to run into the cold night air.

"Marin?" Lucky called out.

"Here," she answered.

She sounded a lot closer to the barn than he wanted her to be, and he spotted her running toward the pasture. She had Noah clutched to her chest, and the little guy was still crying.

Kinley followed Marin, and since Lucky needed to put some distance between the barn and him, he wasn't too far behind. He glanced over his shoulder though and saw something he didn't like.

Howard wasn't anywhere in sight.

Lucky didn't have time to react to that because behind them, the barn exploded into a fireball.

Brenna finally quit struggling, thanks to a chunk of the roof that nearly landed right on them. Lucky latched on to her even harder and raced them across the pasture to safety.

Ahead of him, Marin stopped and looked back. She

was far enough away, he hoped, to avoid being hit with any of the fiery debris. He caught up with Kinley, and the three of them raced to join Marin. Out of breath now and unnerved with adrenaline, they stopped and looked at the blaze that had nearly claimed their lives.

"How dare you endanger my child!" Marin warned Brenna. Her eyes were narrowed, and her breath was coming out in rough jolts.

Lucky checked Noah to make sure he was okay. He appeared to be, despite the crying. They'd been fortunate. A lot could have gone wrong in that barn.

He pulled Marin and Noah into his arms for a short but much needed hug before he turned back around to face Brenna. He was about to add to Marin's warning when he heard the sound of an engine.

Slowly, he looked behind them, fearing what he would see. His fears were confirmed.

A truck was coming right at them.

"It's my father," Marin announced.

The interior truck cab light was on, and the driver's door was partly open, clearly revealing the driver.

"Run," he instructed the others.

However, Lucky didn't move. The man was obviously hell-bent on killing them. Lucky was hell bent on making sure that didn't happen. Noah, Marin and his sister had already been through enough, and this had to end now.

Kinley latched on to Brenna's arm and got her moving.

"Run!" Lucky repeated when Marin stayed put.

He looked at her, to make sure she understood that

he wasn't going to let her and Noah die. She said a lot with that one look. A look that made him realize he would do anything to protect her. That look also made him realize that this could be goodbye.

With the truck closing in on them, she nodded. "I love you," she said. And she turned to run.

I love you.

Powerful words. Words that would have normally shaken him to the core. But he'd have to deal with Marin's admission later. Because right now, he had to do something to stop Howard Sheppard.

Lucky lifted his hand. Took aim at the truck. And waited. Behind him, he could hear Marin running with Noah. His sister and Brenna weren't too far ahead of them. Yet something else to concern him—he didn't want Brenna doing anything stupid.

But for now, he speared all of his attention on Howard.

He watched the truck barrel over the pasture. Howard no doubt had his foot jammed on the accelerator. Pedal to the metal.

Everything inside Lucky stilled. Focused. He adjusted his arm. And when the truck was within range, Lucky double tapped the trigger. The windshield shattered, and Lucky dove to the side so he wouldn't be run over.

He immediately got up and raced into position for round two, so that Howard couldn't get anywhere near Marin and Noah.

But it wasn't necessary.

The truck careened to the left, going right into the

rocky stream. Just yards on the other side, it came to a stop. No brake lights. No signs that the driver had tried to bring the truck under control.

Lucky soon learned why.

With his gun ready, he approached the vehicle. But his vigilance and caution weren't necessary.

Howard was slumped in the seat.

Dead.

"Hell," Lucky cursed.

Now, he was going to have to tell Marin that he'd killed her father.

Chapter Nineteen

The morning sun was too bright, and it glared directly into Marin's eyes.

She didn't move from the glass-encased patio off her bedroom. She couldn't. There seemed to be no energy left in her body so she stayed put on the wicker love seat.

This was the aftermath of a nightmare.

And in some ways, the continuation of one.

Seemingly oblivious to the fact that he'd recently been kidnapped and endangered by Brenna Martel, Noah was playing on a quilt at her feet. He batted at her leg with a small stuffed dog and laughed as if he'd accomplished something phenomenal. Marin couldn't even manage a weak smile in response, though with every fiber of her being, she was thankful that her child hadn't been harmed.

In the bedroom, she could hear the conversations that were going on. Lucky and the sheriff were discussing what had happened. Her grandmother was talking to her mother.

Consoling her.

After all, her mother had only hours ago learned that her husband was a killer and that both her son and husband were dead. That was a lot for anyone to absorb.

Marin, included.

It'd been years since she'd felt real love for her father, and she had already grieved her brother's death a year earlier when she thought he'd been killed. Still, it hurt. It hurt even more that Dexter and her father had been willing to risk her life, Noah's and Lucky's just so they could cover their tracks. It would take a very long time for Marin to get over what had happened. If ever.

"Lucky wanted me to check on you," she heard her grandmother say. She was now in the doorway, examining Marin. "He'll be finished up with the sheriff soon."

"Good." Because she didn't know what else to say, she repeated it.

Her grandmother walked closer and dropped down into the chair next to her. "Your mother says to tell you that she's sorry."

Marin peered into the bedroom. Her mother was no longer there. "Why didn't she tell me herself?"

"The wound's too fresh. Give her time."

Maybe it was her mood or the fact that she didn't trust her mother, but Marin didn't like the sound of that. "I hope that doesn't mean she'll try to get custody of Noah."

"Not a chance. She'll be lucky if she doesn't get jail time for aiding and abetting Dexter. Your brother was a fugitive, and the federal agents aren't happy that she kept his whereabouts a secret from them."

Neither was Marin.

But then, she wasn't pleased about a lot of things.

"What about Lucky?" Marin asked, almost afraid to hear the answer. "Has he said anything about when he'll be leaving?"

"Not to me." Her gran hesitated. "I'm guessing from your tone that you expect him to go?"

Marin didn't trust her voice and settled for a nod. Lucky would have to tend to his sister and tie up the loose ends of this investigation. Without a custody hearing, there was no reason for him to hang around.

Or was there?

So what if she and Lucky had slept together? That didn't obligate him to be part of her life. But God help her, that's what she wanted. Still, she couldn't cling. She'd spent a lifetime being coddled, and if this brush with death had taught her anything, it was that she was strong enough to stand on her own two feet.

She heard the footsteps, glanced in the direction of the sound and saw Lucky making his way toward them. Marin straightened her shoulders and lifted her chin. She doubted that she could completely erase her gloom-and-doom expression, but she tried. She didn't want this conversation to turn into a pity party.

"How's your sister?" Marin asked when Lucky joined them.

"She's fine. She's at the Justice Department office in San Antonio. There won't be any charges filed against her, but she needs to give her statement about what happened the night of the explosion and assist them with the case against Brenna. Once she's done with that, she can leave and get her baby. My nephew," he added, causing a brief smile to bend his mouth.

"Good." Marin winced. It sounded like a token well-wishing. It wasn't.

Looking totally uncomfortable, Lucky stared at her a moment, moved closer and sank down on the floor next to Noah. He immediately got a bop on the forearm from Noah's stuffed dog, and her son giggled.

"Are you playing with your da-da?" her gran asked Noah. She goosed his tummy, causing Noah to laugh even more.

Marin frowned at the question. Her grandmother knew the truth. Lucky and she had lied about, well, pretty much everything—he wasn't Noah's father or her fiancé.

Helen stood. "I think I need a nap. Let me know if you need me to babysit." And with that, she kissed all three of their cheeks and left the room—but not before she winked at Marin.

With her exit came plenty of silence.

Noah volleyed glances between them, trying to figure out what was going on with the sudden silence. Marin wanted to know the same.

"Brenna was arrested, of course," Lucky informed her. He sounded as grim as his expression.

Marin choked back a laugh. "Between your sister and her, maybe we'll learn the truth about what happened at that research facility."

He grunted. "From what Brenna said before they took her away, Dexter couldn't deliver the chemical weapon so he forced her and Kinley to fake their deaths, and then spent the last year trying to eliminate them so there'd be no witnesses as to what he'd done."

Now, it was her turn to make that sound. "And Dexter used your sister as a decoy for the train explosion."

Lucky nodded. "The Justice Department thinks Dexter used a disguise when he got on the train. They'll take a harder look at those surveillance disks."

They'd no doubt take a harder look at all the evidence. But in the end, it would lead them back to Dexter and her father. "I figure that's why Dexter was trying to kill you. Because he knew that between you and Grady Duran, you were close to figuring out the truth."

She paused because she had to and then added, "I'm sorry."

"I'm sorry," Lucky said at the exact moment.

Marin stared at him and blinked. "Why are you sorry? My brother terrorized your sister, forced her to put her child in hiding, and then my father and Dexter tried to murder you."

Lucky held the stare for several moments and then looked away. "I killed your father."

She heard it then. The pain in his voice. It cut her to the bone. Because Lucky was obviously agonizing over something he couldn't have prevented.

"My father didn't give you a choice. And I don't blame you for his death. In fact, if you hadn't killed him, he would have done the same to us. You saved my life, again."

Tears threatened, but Marin blinked them back. She needed to stay strong.

So she could tell Lucky goodbye.

He already had enough guilt without her adding more. The trick was to make this quick. She couldn't make it painless. But she could do Lucky this one last favor.

"As soon as the sheriff gives me the all clear, I'll call a taxi to take me to the airport." She reached for Noah, but he batted her hands away and climbed into Lucky's lap.

Her son grinned up at Lucky. "Da-Da," he said with perfect clarity.

Marin groaned and buried her face in her hands. It was Noah's first word. And it couldn't have come at a worse time.

"I think my grandmother taught him that," Marin said as an apology. She risked looking at Lucky then.

He was glaring at her. "You'll call a taxi to take you to the airport."

It wasn't a question. It was more like a snarl.

"Your rental car is wrecked from the drive-in explosion," she reminded him.

Just then, Noah said, "Da-Da" again. In fact, he began to rattle it off, stringing the syllables together while he snuggled against Lucky.

"You'll call a taxi?"

Both Lucky and Noah gave her accusing stares as if they were waiting. But waiting for what? Marin couldn't give Noah the nod of approval for his Da-Da mantra. Nor could she back down on calling that taxi. She couldn't be clingy. She had to be strong.

Even though her heart was breaking.

Lucky kissed Noah on the forehead and mimicked what her son was saying nonstop. "Da-Da is right." And then Lucky turned those sizzling gray eyes back on Marin. "I might have started out as a replacement father, but as far as Noah and I are concerned, I'm the real deal. Any objections?"

She glanced at her son's happy face and then at Lucky. Not happy, exactly. Hot and riled.

"No objections," she managed to say.

The silence came again.

Marin just sat there. What was she supposed to say or do? The right thing was to give Lucky that out.

Wasn't it?

He had a life, one that hadn't included her before he started investigating Dexter. But then, she'd had a life, too. A life she no longer wanted—it didn't include Lucky.

"You about got it figured out?" Lucky asked.

Marin frowned at his question, which seemed not only eerily insightful, but also like a challenge. Yes, she'd figured out what she wanted. Marin wanted the life in front of her. Lucky as Noah's father. And Lucky as her lover.

No, wait.

She wanted more than that.

The corner of Lucky's mouth lifted. "Count to ten and tell me what you want."

"One," she mumbled. Marin slid down out of the love seat and sat on the floor next to him. She was about to move on to two, but it seemed rather pointless.

"I'm in love with you, Lucky," she confessed. "I don't

want a taxi, and I don't want to go to the airport unless you're with Noah and me."

The other corner of his mouth lifted for a full-fledged smile. "And?"

She leaned in and kissed him. "And I want to be your lover and your wife. I want to marry you."

A chuckle rumbled deep within his chest. "And?"

Marin wasn't sure what he wanted her to say. She'd already poured out her heart. But what she hadn't done was take the ultimate risk. "And I want you to be in love in with me, too."

She held her breath.

Waited.

Heck, she even prayed.

"Then, you have everything you want, Marin. I'm crazy in love with you."

Lucky slid his arm around her neck, pulled her to him and kissed her, hard.

The kiss might have gone on for hours had it not been for Noah. He bopped them with the stuffed dog and laughed when they pulled away from each other.

"Da-Da," Noah announced.

Noah certainly knew a good thing when he saw it. And so did Marin. She pulled her family into her arms and held on tight.

* * * * *

TEXAS PATERNITY *continues in January 2009, only from Delores Fossen and Harlequin Intrigue!*

Here's a sneak peek at
THE CEO'S CHRISTMAS PROPOSITION,
the first in USA TODAY *bestselling author*
Merline Lovelace's HOLIDAYS ABROAD *trilogy*
coming in November 2008.

American Devon McShay is about to get the Christmas surprise of a lifetime when she meets her new client, sexy billionaire Caleb Logan, for the very first time.

Silhouette®
Desire

Available November 2008.

Her breath whistled out in a sigh of relief when he exited Customs. Devon recognized him right away from the newspaper and magazine articles her friend and partner Sabrina had looked up during her frantic prep work.

Caleb John Logan Jr. Thirty-one. Six-two. With jet-black hair, laser-blue eyes and a linebacker's shoulders under his charcoal-gray cashmere overcoat. His jaw-dropping good looks didn't score him any points with Devon. She'd learned the hard way not to trust handsome heartbreakers like Cal Logan.

But he was a client. An important one. And she was willing to give someone who'd served a hitch in the marines before earning a BS from the University of Oregon, an MBA from Stanford and his first million at the ripe old age of twenty-six the benefit of the doubt.

Right up until he spotted the hot-pink pashmina, that is.

Devon knew the flash of color was more visible than the sign she held up with his name on it. So she wasn't surprised when Logan picked her out of the crowd and cut in her direction. She'd just plastered on her best businesswoman smile when he whipped an arm around her waist. The next moment she was sprawled against his cashmere-covered chest.

"Hello, brown eyes."

Swooping down, he covered her mouth with his.

Sheer astonishment kept Devon rooted to the spot for a few seconds while her mind whirled chaotically. Her first thought was that her client had downed a few too many drinks during the long flight. Her second, that he'd mistaken the kind of escort and consulting services her company provided. Her third shoved everything else out of her head.

The man could kiss!

His mouth moved over hers with a skill that ignited sparks at a half-dozen flash points throughout her body. Devon hadn't experienced that kind of spontaneous combustion in a while. A *long* while.

The sparks were still popping when she pushed off his chest, only now they fueled a flush of anger.

"Do you always greet women you don't know with a lip-lock, Mr. Logan?"

A smile crinkled the skin at the corners of his eyes. "As a matter of fact, I don't. That was from Don."

"Huh?"

"He said he owed you one from New Year's Eve two years ago and made me promise to deliver it."

She stared up at him in total incomprehension. Logan hooked a brow and attempted to prompt a non-existent memory.

"He abandoned you at the Waldorf. Five minutes before midnight. To deliver twins."

"I don't have a clue who or what you're..."

Understanding burst like a water balloon.

"Wait a sec. Are you talking about Sabrina's old boyfriend? Your buddy, who's now an ob-gyn doc?"

It was Logan's turn to look startled. He recovered faster than Devon had, though. His smile widened into a rueful grin.

"I take it you're not Sabrina Russo."

"No, Mr. Logan, I am *not*."

* * * * *

Be sure to look for
THE CEO'S CHRISTMAS PROPOSITION
by Merline Lovelace.
Available in November 2008
wherever books are sold,
including most bookstores, supermarkets,
drugstores and discount stores.

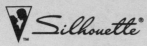

Silhouette®
Romantic
SUSPENSE

**Sparked by Danger,
Fueled by Passion.**

Lindsay McKenna
Susan Grant

Mission: Christmas

Celebrate the holidays with a pair
of military heroines and their daring men
in two romantic, adventurous stories
from these bestselling authors.

Featuring:

"The Christmas Wild Bunch"
by *USA TODAY* bestselling author
Lindsay McKenna
and

"Snowbound with a Prince"
by *New York Times* bestselling author
Susan Grant

Available November wherever books are sold.

REQUEST YOUR FREE BOOKS!

2 FREE NOVELS
PLUS 2
FREE GIFTS!

 HARLEQUIN®

INTRIGUE®

Breathtaking Romantic Suspense

YES! Please send me 2 FREE Harlequin Intrigue® novels and my 2 FREE gifts (gifts are worth about $10). After receiving them, if I don't wish to receive any more books, I can return the shipping statement marked "cancel." If I don't cancel, I will receive 6 brand-new novels every month and be billed just $4.24 per book in the U.S. or $4.99 per book in Canada, plus 25¢ shipping and handling per book and applicable taxes, if any*. That's a savings of close to 15% off the cover price! I understand that accepting the 2 free books and gifts places me under no obligation to buy anything. I can always return a shipment and cancel at any time. Even if I never buy another book from Harlequin, the two free books and gifts are mine to keep forever.

182 HDN EEZ7   382 HDN EEZK

Name	(PLEASE PRINT)	
Address		Apt. #
City	State/Prov.	Zip/Postal Code

Signature (if under 18, a parent or guardian must sign)

Mail to the **Harlequin Reader Service:**
IN U.S.A.: P.O. Box 1867, Buffalo, NY 14240-1867
IN CANADA: P.O. Box 609, Fort Erie, Ontario L2A 5X3

Not valid to current subscribers of Harlequin Intrigue books.

Want to try two free books from another line?
Call 1-800-873-8635 or visit www.morefreebooks.com.

* Terms and prices subject to change without notice. N.Y. residents add applicable sales tax. Canadian residents will be charged applicable provincial taxes and GST. Offer not valid in Quebec. This offer is limited to one order per household. All orders subject to approval. Credit or debit balances in a customer's account(s) may be offset by any other outstanding balance owed by or to the customer. Please allow 4 to 6 weeks for delivery. Offer available while quantities last.

Your Privacy: Harlequin is committed to protecting your privacy. Our Privacy Policy is available online at www.eHarlequin.com or upon request from the Reader Service. From time to time we make our lists of customers available to reputable third parties who may have a product or service of interest to you. If you would prefer we not share your name and address, please check here. ☐

HI08R

MARRIED BY CHRISTMAS

Playboy billionaire Elijah Vanaldi has discovered
he is guardian to his small orphaned nephew.
But his reputation makes some people question
his ability to be a father. He knows he must
fight to protect the child, and he'll do anything
it takes. Ainslie Farrell is jobless, homeless and
desperate—and when Elijah offers her a position
in his household she simply can't refuse....

Available in November

HIRED: THE ITALIAN'S
CONVENIENT MISTRESS
by
CAROL MARINELLI

Book #29

COMING NEXT MONTH

#1095 CHRISTMAS AWAKENING by Ann Voss Peterson
A Holiday Mystery at Jenkins Cove
The ghost of Christmas present looms over Brandon Drake when his
butler's daughter returns to Drake House. Can Marie Leonard and the
scarred millionaire find answers in their shared past that will enable
them to catch her father's killer?

#1096 MIRACLE AT COLTS RUN CROSS by Joanna Wayne
Four Brothers of Colts Run Cross
When their twins are kidnapped, Nick Ridgely and Becky Collingsworth
face the biggest crisis in their marriage yet. Will the race to save
their children bring them closer in time for an old-fashioned Texas
Christmas?

#1097 SILENT NIGHT SANCTUARY by Rita Herron
Guardian Angel Investigations
When Leah Holden's seven-year-old sister goes missing, she turns to
detective Kyle McKinney. To reunite this family, Kyle will do anything to
find the child, even if it means crossing the line with the law...and with
Leah.

#1098 CHRISTMAS CONFESSIONS by Kathleen Long
Hunted by a killer who's never been caught, Abby Conroy's world is
sent into a tailspin, which only police detective Gage McDermont can
pull her out of. One thing is certain: this holiday season's going to be
murder...

#1099 KANSAS CITY CHRISTMAS by Julie Miller
The Precinct: Brotherhood of the Badge
Edward Kincaid has no reason to celebrate Christmas—until he begins
playing reluctant bodyguard to Dr. Holly Robinson. Now, the M.E. who can
bust the city's biggest case wide open might also be the only one able to
crack Edward's tough shell.

#1100 NICK OF TIME by Elle James
Santa's missing from the North Pole and his daughter, Mary Christmas,
can't save the holiday by herself. It's up to cowboy and danger-junkie
Nick St. Clair to find the jolly ol' fellow in time for the holidays, before
Christmas is done for as he knows it....

www.eHarlequin.com

HICNM1008BPA